THE MUSICAL ™

Based on the Board Game by Parker Brothers

Book by
Peter DePietro

Lyrics by
Tom Chiodo

Music by
Galen Blum
Wayne Barker
Vinnie Martucci

SAMUEL FRENCH, INC.
45 WEST 25TH STREET   NEW YORK 10010
7623 SUNSET BOULEVARD   HOLLYWOOD 90046
LONDON   *TORONTO*

Amateurs wishing to arrange for the production of CLUE: The Musical must make application to SAMUEL FRENCH, INC., at 45 West 25th Street, New York, N. Y. 10010, giving the following particulars:

(1) The name of the town and theatre or hall of the proposed production.
(2) The maximum seating capacity of the theatre or hall.
(3) Scale of ticket prices.
(4) The number of performances intended, and the dates thereof.
(5) Indicate whether you will use an orchestration or simply a piano.

Upon receipt of these particulars SAMUEL FRENCH, INC., will quote terms and availability.

Stock royalty quoted on application to SAMUEL FRENCH, INC., 45 West 25th Street, New York, N.Y. 10010.

For all other rights than those stipulated above apply to SAMUEL FRENCH, INC. 45 West 25th Street, New York, NY 10010.

An orchestration consisting of:

Piano Conductor Score (includes Synthesizer)
Cello
Percussion
8 Vocal Chorus Books

will be loaned two months prior to the production ONLY on receipt of the royalty quoted for all performances, the rental fee and a refundable deposit. The deposit will be refunded on the safe return to SAMUEL FRENCH, INC. of all materials loaned for the production.

Printed in U.S.A.

ISBN 0 573 66365 3

AUTHOR'S NOTES:

GAME PLAY Upon entering the theatre, each audience member receives a playing form, with detailed instructions on how and when to use the form. This is important, as the verbal instructions given in the script are general. (A sample form can be found in the Production Manual, information below.) They each also receive a small writing instrument. (Golf pencils work well.) House lights should be illuminated whenever a clue is given, so that the audience can document the information. This is stipulated in the script

SCRIPT VARIATIONS The script is designed so that each time CLUE is performed, there are variations in the text. These text options are incorporated into the script. The option delivered in a given performance is determined by the cards selected by the audience.

SET The design should be simple, creative and functional. The core of the set is a series of six four-sided towers on wheel, which configure in sundry ways to form representations of each of the rooms of Boddy Manor. These towers should be constructed so that they are very mobile and easily moved by the actors. It is important to the concept of the musical that the characters move the set pieces during scene transitions, with stylized staging. The suggestion here is that the characters, locked in a game, are moving the pieces necessary for game play. For seating and table surfaces, use a single chair and rolling table unit for all scenes. Creative and simple ornamentation can make the table appropriate for all the rooms in which it is used.

COSTUMES All characters should be costumed in their signature color. No single time period should be evident in the overall design. The look should be timeless.

PROPS Weapons and cards are designed in the style of the board game but are oversized. Largeness is important.

MISCELLANEOUS *CLUE The Musical* is performed without an intermission

PRODUCTION MANUAL Please note that more detailed production information, in addition to what appears above, is available in the CLUE: The Musical Production Manual, available through Samuel French, Inc. Contact them at 45 West 25 Street, NY NY 10010. Tel: 212-206-8990

For
Dan, Wendy and Manfred

CLUE The Musical Cast
(In Order of Appearance)

MR. BODDY   Charismatic, handsome, playful host; 30s; soaring baritone/tenor

MRS. PEACOCK   Acerbic, manipulative, sexy socialite; plays 40s; mezzo with belt

PROFESSOR PLUM   Astute intellectual with a wry sense of humor; plays 30s-40s; baritone

MISS SCARLET   Shrewd, very attractive vixen; 20s; wide vocal range with belt

COLONEL MUSTARD   Pompous, randy military man; plays 40s-50s; baritone

MRS. WHITE   Fun-loving cockney maid, portrayed by a man; plays 40s-50s; wide vocal range

MR. GREEN   Slick, handsome wheeler-dealer; 20s; baritone/tenor

DETECTIVE   Hard-nosed, snappy, humorous female; 30s; interesting singing voice

(*Note*: Mrs. Peacock, Professor Plum, Miss Scarlet, Colonel Mustard, Mrs. White and Mr. Green are collectively referred to as the SUSPECTS.)

TIME: Now

PLACE: Boddy Manor

MUSICAL NUMBERS

THE GAME.. Mr. Boddy, Suspects

LIFE IS A BOWL OF PITS... Mrs. White

EVERDAY DEVICES.................. Miss Scarlet and Mr. Green with
    Colonel Mustard, Professor Plum, Mrs. White, Mrs Peacock

ONCE A WIDOW... Mrs. Peacock

CORRIDORS AND HALLS........................... Mr. Boddy, Suspects

THE MURDER.. Mr. Boddy, Suspects

AFTER THE MURDER (THE GAME Reprise)............... Suspects

SHE HASN'T GOT A CLUE...Suspects

EVERYDAY DEVICES (Reprise)..................................... Suspects

SEDUCTION DEDUCTION................. Professor Plum, Detective

FOUL WEATHER FRIEND.. Suspects

DON'T BLAME ME ....Entire Cast

THE FINAL CLUE...Mr. Boddy, Suspects

THE GAME (Finale)..Mr. Boddy, Suspects

SHE HASN'T GOT A CLUE (Reprise)/Bows................Entire Cast

CLUE
The Musical

(As the audience enters the theatre, they receive playing forms and pencils, with which to play the game. A full-sized curtain or lighted gobo prominently displays the CLUE logo.)

OVERTURE

(BODDY enters.)

BODDY.
Good evening, Ladies and Gentlemen,
Boddy, Mr. Boddy is my name.
Welcome to my home, Boddy Manor.
Of tonight's event I am the planner—
This fun and folly known as a game

(With a flash of BODDY's hand, an elaborate oversized rendition of the CLUE game board appears.)

*(BODDY sings **THE GAME**.)*

BODDY.
HERE INSIDE THE BOX
A DECK OF CARDS
A PAIR OF DICE TO TOSS

(BODDY speaks the following lines.)

The premise of the game is simple:
Kill me—with one weapon, in one room.

You won't rest easily
'Til I rest permanently.
Ah, the immeasurable joy of my doom.

(He continues singing.)

FIND SIX ROOMS INSIDE
A PLACE TO HIDE
A PLACE TO PLAY A GAME
MURDER IS ITS NAME
YOU CHOOSE THE CARDS
YOU PLAY IT HARD
BUT ONLY ONE CAN WIN
MURDER IS THE BILL OF FARE
NOW YOU'LL SEE MOTIVE EVERYWHERE
SO LET THE GAME BEGIN

SIX WEAPONS PASS FROM HAND TO HAND WITH PASSION
SIX SUSPECTS FROM SQUARE ONE ARE ON THE RUN
LET'S MEET THEM NOW AND HEAR THE TALES THEY
            FASHION
BE CAUTIOUS
FROM HERE IT'S ALL OR NONE FOR MURDER ONE

(PEACOCK enters.)

PEACOCK. I am Mrs. Peacock: well-known, well-traveled and well-preserved. I am the rose of the Peacock Family and Chairperson of the Board of Peacock Enterprises, a position I acquired with the death of my first husband, Anthony. My second husband, Neville, gave me an authentic Renoir; Vincenzo, my third, my villa in Capri; my fourth, a 10-carat diamond ring. I've forgotten my fifth completely. He gave me ... nothing. I'm happy to say I'm a newlywed again. Mr. Boddy recently became my sixth. I have wealth. I have power. *(Beat.)* I have Ivana Trump's plastic surgeon.

(Sings.)

IF I'M THE ONE THEY CHOOSE TO BE THE KILLER
POOR DARLING, THIS MEANS YOU'RE MY SIXTH TO DIE.
  BODDY.
THEN PROMISE ME YOU'LL MAKE SURE IT'S A THRILLER
  PEACOCK.
I WILL, BUT I'LL NEED SOMEONE TO BE MY ALIBI

(PLUM enters.)

  PLUM. I am Professor Plum. BA, MA, PhD ... that's me. I am an author by trade, an intellect by birth and an American by choice. You see, I was born in London, raised in New York, attended Oxford and years later became part of the British Think Tank in the States. It was in Washington I met Mr. Boddy. He was a lobbyist for the oil industry. He asked me to ghost write a book for him about government involvement in the oil industry, for a handsome fee. Indeed, I agreed. As Somerset Maughm said: "Money is like a sixth sense ... *(Beat.)* You can't make use of the other five without it."

(Sings.)

TO MASTERMIND A CRIME IS QUITE FULFILLING
TO EXECUTE WAS NEVER MY STRONG SUIT
THE MASTERMIND WILL ALWAYS GET TOP BILLING
THE CORPSE IS A NAMELESS BODY PLAINLY DRESSED TO
    BOOT
  BODDY.
'TIL THE DEED IT DONE
I'M GAME FOR EVERYONE
  BODDY and PLUM.
MURDER IS OUR BILL OF FARE
AND YOU'LL SEE MOTIVE EVERYWHERE
BUT ONLY ONE CAN WIN
  PLUM.
ONLY ONE CAN WIN
  PEACOCK.
ONLY ONE CAN WIN

(SCARLET enters.)

SCARLET. I'm Miss Scarlet. I'm an actress ... well, a singer ... no, more like a performer. You know, I do it all. Or so that's what my men friends tell me. Now one knows this, but I first met Mr. Boddy, when I was performing in Las Vegas. I opened for a dog juggling act, which played every Tuesday at three a.m. at Billy's Lonestar Bar, Grill and Casino. Mr. Boddy was in Vegas on Business. He saw my show, *loved* it, and asked if I'd give him an encore in his hotel room. Well, you know me ... *(Beat.)* I love an audience.

(Sings.)

LAST TIME WE PLAYED THE GAME I HAD TO SHOOT
        YOU
THE TRIGGER JAMMED, I NEARLY MISSED MY CUE

(MUSTARD enters.)

MUSTARD. Colonel Mustard here. I've stormed bunkers, pillaged barricades and triumphed in war. Not with might. But with imagination. See, this soldier never had the opportunity to serve in the armed forces, because of legislation drafted by Senator Boddy, Mr. Boddy's father. It bans from the military any person who has the disease which causes people to mistake humans for inanimate objects: Non-identifyusitis. People live quite normally with the ailment, 'til they're excited and their blood pressure increases. Then your neighbor becomes a Volkswagon, your son a toaster—you get the idea. Shortly after the bill was passed, Senator Boddy mysteriously died. *(Beat, then sly.)* Now Mr. Boddy calls me Dad.

(Sings.)

DO YOU RECALL THE LAST TIME THAT I KILLED YOU?
I BEAT YOU SILLY WITH A CANDLESTICK
    BODDY.
BUT I RECALL YOU STRUCK ME WITH A LEAD PIPE

MUSTARD.
YES, THAT'S RIGHT
TONIGHT PERHAPS TONIGHT I'LL TRY MY NEW ROPE
    TRICK

(WHITE enters.)

MRS. WHITE. Me name is Mrs. White. I hate the Mrs. part, but that's what I'm called by Mr. Boddy, who I lives with, as I'm his housekeeper, actually his cook and housekeeper, but he don't pay me enough to be called both, so I say I'm just his housekeeper, and I don't mean to say I lives with 'im, 'cause I got me own teeny, tiny room in the basement, where I sleep on a thin, thin, thin mattress on a cot what ain't fit for prisoners in a jail cell. And the food! I get scraps, leftovers tasteless, gristly stuff the dog won't eat. And I works seven days a week—seven long, hard days with no rest for me weary bones, me weary muscles, me weary hands, feet, eyes, nose, hair. *(Beat.)* I need a drink.

(Sings.)

IN MYST'RIES THEY ALL BLAME THE MAID OR BUTLER
    BODDY.
BUT WE DON'T HAVE A BUTLER HERE TO BLAME
    WHITE.
AND IF THE COPPERS COME A HUNTIN' FOR ME
I'M READY
A JAIL HOUSE FULL O' BLOKES FOR ME TO TAME

(GREEN enters.)

MR. GREEN. Green's the name. Money's my game. I'm sultan of the stock market, king of commodities—an entrepreneur. I got me a national chain of beauty salons called Teasin' Your Blues Away; I own the world's most popular discount air carrier, Pennies in Heaven; and I'm part of a joint venture, with Mr. Boddy, which specializes in the restoration of ancient monuments, called Colossal Nips and Tucks. Our recent project is the Great Pyramids. We're gonna protect them from the elements by covering them with vinyl siding. What a concept: sandstone-colored siding that blends into the stone, so you don't even know it's there. *(Beat.)* I'm a genius.

SIX SUSPECTS.

SIX WEAPONS PASS FROM HAND
  TO HAND WITH PASSION
SIX SUSPECTS FROM SQUARE ONE
  WE'RE ON THE RUN
YOU'VE ME US NOW AND HEAR
  THE TALES WE FASHIONED

BODDY.

NOW IT'S ALL OR
  NONE
AND WE PLAY TO
  WIN

PLUM.
BE CAUTIOUS
MUSTARD.
INTREPID
GREEN.
CONNIVING
WHITE.
CONTRIVING
SCARLET.
SEDUCTIVE
PEACOCK.
ELUSIVE
ALL.
SO NOW YOU PLAY OUR LITTLE GAME OF MURDER
YOU TRY YOUR BEST AND PLAY THE GAME TO WIN
AND NOW MATTER IF YOU LAND ON TOP OR BOTTOM
YOU'VE PLAYED IT
AND NOW IT'S TIME TO PLAY THE GAME AGAIN
THE GAME HAS NOW BEGUN
SIX SUSPECTS ON THE RUN
FROM HERE IT'S ALL OR NONE FOR MURDER ONE

(ALL end in a tableau.)

BODDY. *(Speaks.)*
Tonight, we won't save the world from ruin
We won't get a Nobel Prize
We won't win lottery jackpots

We will encounter some crackpots
Loony antics and clues to scrutinize
GREEN. Crackpots. How'dya like that? He called us crackpots.
PEACOCK. Take a look around. You don't find sane people living in a two-dimensional world made of yellow blocks and paint-by-number rooms.
BODDY.
Ladies and Gentlemen,
You will determine the conclusion of the game—
The suspect, the weapon and the room are essential.
You will do this by selecting cards from three decks
and placing them in this envelope marked "Confidential".

(BODDY motions to the Confidential envelope, on display as part of the set.)

BODDY. (Cont.)
There are six options in each of three categories.
Six, six, six ... hmm ... very interesting.
There are two-hundred and sixteen potential finales,
But on only *one* is our game resting.
MUSTARD. Here we go again.
GREEN. The slap of the cards.
PEACOCK. The crash of the die.
PLUM. The sticky fingers grasping me.
SCARLET. *(Pleased.)* The strong fingers grasping me.
WHITE. You always get the strong fingers!

(SUSPECTS: Ad lib.)

BODDY. Excuse me. *(He presents Deck No. 1.)* The first deck has cards representing each of the murder suspects ...

(BODDY displays each card, as he announces the names. CHARACTERS exit as their name is mentioned.)

Mrs. Peacock, Mr. Green, Miss Scarlet, Colonel Mustard, Professor Plum and Mrs. White.

(Beat. BODDY cuts the deck of cards,as he continues.)

Before the show began
We recruited three volunteers—
Each to select one card.
I ask them now to take the stage;
I ask with humblest regard.

(BODDY addresses the first volunteer, fanning the cards, face down.)

BODDY. I would like you to select the murderer by picking a single card and placing it in front of you like this.

(BODDY demonstrates, making sure that no one onstage or in the audience can see the face of the card.)

BODDY. (cont.) The second deck contains one card for each of the rooms in Boddy Manor, where the murder might take place: the kitchen, the ballroom, the lounge, the billiard room, the conservatory and the study. Please pick the room.

(BODDY approaches the next volunteer to select a card, reiterating placement instructions, if necessary.)

BODDY. (Cont.) The third deck has cards fo reach of the weapons that might be used in the murder: the candlestick, the rope, the lead pipe, the revolver, the knife and the wrench. Please choose the weapon.

(The last volunteer chooses. BODDY thanks the volunteers, as he collects the three cards they chose, and dismisses them. Then adds...)

BODDY. Let's have a round of applause for our volunteers.

(BODDY places the envelope on a grand display in full view of the audience. Here it remains, illuminated, for the duration of the show.)

BODDY.
Ladies and Gentlemen,
In this envelope is the key to our destiny,
For in it lies the answer to the mystery.

(BODDY presents the cards.)

BODDY.
We find ourselves in an interesting place:
The ending is chosen before we begin.
What then is the objective
From a player's perspective
To solve the mystery and ultimately win?

Your goal is to figure out what's in the envelope:
Whodunit, with what weapon, in what room.
You arrive at this conclusion
By deducing the solution
From clues I will give you once we resume.

There are two rounds of clues that will assist you:
Before my death, Round One; After, Round Two.
Participation in the game is purely by choice.

(He presents a sample playing form.)
If you play, use the playing form you received.
Document the information I reveal with each clue
Then eliminate items with no value perceived
Thus, you find where, how and who.

Our official light-up board will assist in your endeavor,
So when it lights, heed its report with pleasure.
We'll be anxious to see at the end of the game
If your answer and ours are one in the same.

(With the following line, BODDY refers to the envelope.)

BODDY.
Now we start our journey to arrive at this end.

To all suspicious doing diligently attend.

(Set changes to the kitchen.)

BODDY.
Round One begins in the kitchen with shrieks of woe
From a disgruntled worker, less friend than foe.

(MRS. WHITE is preparing a meal. She flails about a roast on a large fork, whacking it with a lead pipe.)

WHITE. "Make sure the roast is succulent and tender," he said. Make sure the salad is gently tossed." I've a good mind to burn his roast and rip his salad apart. I've a good mind to ...

(BODDY walks into the scene.)

BODDY. Mrs. White ... *(Startled, she drops the roast.)* What are you doing!?
WHITE. *(With lead pipe in hand.)* Tenderizin' the roast.
BODDY. With a lead pipe?
WHITE. *(Retrieves the roast.)* Uh, huh.

(Use the following dialogue in italics only if MRS. WHITE has been chosen as the killer.)

BODDY. *(Magically presents a piece of sheet music.) Mrs. White, what's this?*
WHITE. *(Defensive.) Where'd you get that?*
BODDY. *In your chamber. (Pause. WHITE looks dumbfounded and does not respond.) It's sheet music. (Sly.) What are you going with sheet music to Beethoven's Fifth Symphony?*
WHITE. *(Caught, she contrives and answer.) Uhm ... well ... I'm looking to add some culture to me life.*

(WHITE fixes an undergarment.)

BODDY. Just make sure dinner preparations are completed, according to my specifications.

(BODDY starts to exit. WHITE follows.)

WHITE. I think you and me is gotta talk, Mr. Boddy. About me position.

BODDY. You are my chief domestic, Mrs. White. There is nothing else to discuss.

WHITE. Me wages. And the raise I ain't got in ...

BODDY. Are you forgetting that I paid the bail required by the court to free your step-son Nigel?

WHITE. *(Sarcastic.)* And I'm ever so grateful. *(BODDY looks with reprimanding eyes.)* Sir.

BODDY. Nigel would still be behind bars awaiting his trial for Grand Larceny, if it weren't for my generous offering.

WHITE. More than generous, Sir. But workin' all these hours to pay you back is takin' its toll. Me body feels like I just had a marathon night with at troop of blokes from the Royal Navy.

BODDY. Mrs. White!

WHITE. Yeah, you're right. A night with sailors would've at least put a smile on me face.

BODDY. Mrs. White, I want dinner ready in one hour. You are to notify all my guests, when dinner is served. And, after serving it, you are to report to your chamber, until I summon you. Is that understood?

WHITE. Aye, aye, Sir!

BODDY. *(Aside to audience.)* I knew she'd see things my way.

(BODDY exits.)

WHITE. He's the bloody knot in me knittin' yarn, he is. What I need is a new position, with a respectful employer. Unfortunately, at my age there ain't many offers.

(WHITE sings LIFE IS A BOWL OF PITS.)

WHITE.
YOUR LIFE IS A BOWL OF CHERRIES
WHEN ALL THE PIECES FIT
BUT WHEN YOU'RE SCRAMBLIN' TO SURVIVE
LIFE IS A BOWL OF PITS

I'M EV'RYBODY'S DOOR MAT
TO WIPE THEIR FEET UPON
MISTER BODDY RULES ME LIFE
HE RUNS ME FROM DUSK 'TIL DAWN

HIS CARROTS AND HIS BEANS
MUST BE NOUVELLE CUISINE
I AIN'T NO GALLOPING GOURMET
AND FOR A PARTING SHOT
THE POT ROAST WENT TO POT
HE'LL TAKE IT FROM ME TAKE-HOME PAY

M'LIFE AIN'T A BOWL OF CHERRIES
NONE OF THE PIECES FIT
I'M ALWAYS SCRAMBLIN' TO SURVIVE
LIFE IS A BOWL OF PITS

BUT DESTINY SERVED ME LEFTOVERS
INSTEAD OF AN ELEGANT MEAL
IT COULD HAVE BEEN LOBSTERS AND CHAMPAGNE
A MINK COAT AND AUTOMOBILE

BUT I MARRIED BENEATH ME STATION
THE BUTCHER WAS WHO KNOCKED ME UP
AND WE HAD A SON
OUR SON WAS A BUM
IT'S COST ME THE BEST OF ME LIFE

AS MISTER BODDY'S SERVANT
I'M VERY MUCH MALIGNED
HE SURE AIN'T MUCH TO SING ABOUT BUT
GOOD WORK IS HARD TO FIND

NOW HE DON'T EVEN NOTICE
WHEN EVERYTHING RUNS SWELL
HE'LL TREAT ME LIKE I'M SOMEONE WHEN
IT FREEZES UP IN HELL

HE'S GOT NO GRATITUDE
HE'S GOT ME ALL UNGLUED!
I FEAR I'LL STAB INSTEAD OF SLICE

I'LL HACK INSTEAD OF DICE
I'LL BLUDGEON THE BEEF STEW
A MAIN COURSE WORTH THE WAIT
ME MASTER ON A PLATE!

(Mrs. WHITE, vowing revenge, brandishes knives. BODDY appears
  in the shadows and mimes WHITE's actions, inferring that he is
  controlling the action.)

CHOP THIS
TRIM THE FAT

CARVE THIS
IN NOTHING FLAT

MINCE THIS
TOSS THAT

(BODDY exits.)

   WHITE. (Cont. singing.)
BUT LIFE IS A BOWL OF CHERRIES
WHEN ALL OF THE PIECES FIT
I'M DREAMIN' AND I'M SCHEMIN'
THAT SOMEDAY I'LL ARRIVE
I'M ALWAYS SCRAMBLIN' TO SURVIVE
AND WHAT I SAY IS TRUE
LIFE ON THE WHOLE
LIFE IS A BOWL OF PITS

(BODDY enters as House Lights are illuminated. WHITE poses during the following clue.)

BODDY.
Clue Number One:
In the kitchen with the knife was Mrs. White
Who flailed the gleaming blade with might.
She handled the pipe adroitly, too.
One/None* of these weapons is an answer for you.

(*Recite that which applies, according to what rests inside the Confidential envelope.)
(House lights fade out, as Set changes to the Billiard Room.)

BODDY. (Cont.)
Next in the billiard room business goes awry.
When wheeling and dealing can't conceal a lie.

(BODDY steps aside and observes. Having entered, GREEN is shooting pool in the dim light of a candle, positioned in the candle stick.)

GREEN. Four ball corner pocket. Six ball side ...

(BODDY walks into scene.)

BODDY. Good evening, Mr. Green.
GREEN. Hey, how's it goin?
BODDY. The room is dark, even for you. Wouldn't you say?
GREEN. Six of one, half-pound the other.

(BODDY waves his hand and the lights brighten. Music accent. This is unseen by GREEN who concentrates on his next billiards shot.)

GREEN. *(Looks up.)* You in for a game?

(GREEN now notices the light is brighter.)

BODDY. No, thank you. *(To audience.)* I'm already involved in a game.

(Use the following dialogue in italics only if MR. GREEN has been chosen as the killer.)

    BODDY. (Magically presents a piece of sheet music.) Mr. Green, what's this?
    GREEN. (Surprised. Defensive.) Where'd you get that?
    BODDY. In your chamber. (Pause. GREEN looks dumbfounded and does not respond.) It's sheet music. (Sly.) What are you doing with sheet music to Beethoven's Fifth Symphony?
    GREEN. (Stuck, he contrives an answer.) Oh, that ... uhm ... it's for a new venture of mine: a bar with exotic dancers that plays only classical music. It's called Babe-thovens.

(GREEN forces an unconvincing smile.)

BODDY. Do you have the Egyptian deposit for Colossal Nips and Tucks?
GREEN. Not yet, but the government loved our proposal and has given solid verbal commitment, and the check will be cut soon, real soon.
BODDY. That's not true.
GREEN. Sure, it is. They said we'd get the deposit as soon as ...
BODDY. You're lying. I spoke to Yusef abdul Rakbek just yesterday. The check was already delivered to you. And a little research shows that your bank account is now half a million dollars fatter than two days ago.
GREEN. My great aunt Peoria died. A little thank you for being a model nephew.
BODDY. Mr. Green ...
GREEN. No, really. The poor thing was confined to a wheel chair, was crazy and had a removable glass eye. I'd go over and push her around the living room so she could play marbles with it.
BODDY. Mr. Green, I want the correct amount deposited in the Nips and Tucks account immediately.
GREEN. Hey bud, you're walkin' on thin water.

BODDY. Failure to do so will result in legal action brought against you.

GREEN. Go ahead, sue me. You got nothin'. *(Accusatory.)* You're lookin' for a needle in a backpack.

(BODDY reacts front. GREEN poses for the following clue. House Lights up.)

BODDY.
Clue Number Two:
Exhibited in that telling scene—
Billiard room, candle stick and Mr. Green.
None/One/Two of these is/is/are worth remembering,
when you begin your conjecturing.

(Set changes to Ballroom, and House Lights fade out.)

BODDY. (Cont.)
Now in the ballroom a reunion takes place.
Here there's a dubious past to embrace.

(BODDY steps aside and observes. Having entered, PEACOCK is gazing out a window. MUSTARD enters, sneaks up behind her and covers her eyes.)

MUSTARD. A strange place to find you ... in a ballroom *alone.*
PEACOCK. *(Surprised.)* Colonel Mustard!
MUSTARD. How did you know?
PEACOCK. That unquestionable tone of adolescence. *(Turns to him.)* Are you a guest for the weekend?
MUSTARD. No, just here for the evening—a stop-over on my way to a very important affair.
PEACOCK. *(Referring to his mustard-colored costume.)* Are you going to an engagement for Grey Poupon or French's Golden?
MUSTARD. My dear, you haven't changed a bit. You're still that same feisty woman I once adored.
PEACOCK. *(Reminiscing.)* You and me. Oh, that was ... husbands ago.

MUSTARD. Remember when we were passionate friends?

PEACOCK. *(Playfully sexual.)* True allies.

MUSTARD. Hoo-ooh-ooh. Hey, let's play like we did that first night in Monaco. Let's play my favorite.

PEACOCK. Not Custer's Last Stand. *(Beat.)* He never stands very long.

MUSTARD. No, The Storming of Normandy.

PEACOCK. Send in the troops!

MUSTARD. Ten-hut! Europe 1939. Hitler unleashes his wrath. *(MUSTARD retrieves an over-sized map, magically presented by BODDY. He unrolls it and takes a strong stance, as he and PEA-COCK engage in a game, in which their hands and feet end up inter-twined in a playfully sexual way.)* Left foot, Czechoslovakia.

PEACOCK. Right foot, Poland.

MUSTARD. Left hand, Denmark.

PEACOCK. Left hand, Norway.

MUSTARD. Right foot, Holland.

PEACOCK. Right hand, Belgium.

MUSTARD. Right foot, France. D-Day! *(Sound effects accompany musical accompaniment, as MUSTARD and PEACOCK become more intertwined.)* Brigades ...

PEACOCK. Thrust! Artillery ...

MUSTARD. Explodes!

MUSTARD and **PEACOCK.** *(Ad-lib, then ...)* Victory!

(MUSTARD ends up in a comedic, compromising position. There is a pause.)

PEACOCK. Colonel, what is it?

MUSTARD. *(Still bent over.)* My back. My back is stuck.

PEACOCK. What?!

MUSTARD. My plastic vertebrae are jammed. *(Pain hits.)* Aaaaaah!

(MUSTARD drops PEACOCK onto the floor.)

PEACOCK. Plastic vertebrae?!

MUSTARD. War wound.

PEACOCK. What should I do?

MUSTARD. Take my hand, stand on my toes and pull.

PEACOCK. I can't get you up.

MUSTARD. You certainly can. *(Beat.)* On the count of three. One, two, three ...

(PEACOCK pulls MUSTARD up. He grimaces with pain and ends up in a strangely contorted position.)

PEACOCK. Now what?

MUSTARD. One good yank, and I'll straighten up. Pull.

PEACOCK. *(Wry.)* Pull what?

MUSTARD. My shoulders. Pull my shoulders and my back will straighten.

PEACOCK. Here goes. *(PEACOCK comically straightens MUSTARD's back. BODDY enters, unseen by them, and tosses the revolver between PEACOCK and MUSTARD, then exits.)* Colonel, what's that?

(MUSTARD takes it.)

MUSTARD. A revolver.

PEACOCK. I know that. Why is it on your person?

MUSTARD. An old military habit. Got to be prepared. Got to have your pistol loaded and ready to fire. The enemy is everywhere.

PEACOCK. Colonel, I am no enemy.

(PEACOCK grabs MUSTARD and maneuvers him into a dipped embrace, lips locked. BODDY enters.)

BODDY. Colonel Mustard, I want you off the premises immediately.

PEACOCK. *(To BODDY.)* You don't understand.

MUSTARD. *I* don't understand. I was just kissing a rake.

BODDY. I want you out. *(Aside to audience.)* I love my job.

MUSTARD. *(Stern, yet confused.)* Need I remind you that when my mother ... your wife ... my wife ... your ... died, I became owner of this manor, and that my generosity allows you to take up residence.

BODDY. *My mother* may have left you Boddy Manor. But she did not leave you my wife.

MUSTARD. *(Confused.)* Your wife? Where's your wife? Listen, you better put that rake away. That thing has sharp teeth! *(To BODDY.)* I'll finish with you later. Good night.

(MUSTARD fumbles trying to make a grand exit, then regains composure.)

(Use the following dialogue in italics only if COLONEL MUSTARD has been chosen as the killer.)

BODDY. *(Magically presents a piece of sheet music.)* Colonel Mustard, what's this?

MUSTARD. *(Surprised, defensive.) Where'd you get that?*

BODDY. *In your chamber. (Pause. MUSTARD looks dumbfounded and does not respond.) It's sheet music. (Sly.) What are you doing with sheet music to Beethoven's Fifth Symphony?*

MUSTARD. *How dare you abscond my personal effects. This is war!!*

(MUSTARD storms out.)

PEACOCK. I'm going to the Lounge for a cocktail and then to the Conservatory ... for a moment alone ... with the plants!

(PEACOCK and MUSTARD, who reenters, pose for clue. BODDY takes CS. House Lights up.)

BODDY.
Clue Number Three:
Revolver, ballroom, Mustard, Peacock—
Are they the key to the mystery lock?
Spouse and parent—both savvy and wise
Chooses one/neither of them I strongly advise.
Revolver, ballroom—weapon and space;
One/Both/Neither will help strengthen your case.

(Set changes to the Lounge, as House Lights fade out.)

BODDY. (Cont.)
Now in the lounge more motive is forming
In tandem with some sly brainstorming.

(House lights down. SCARLET is preparing an exotic cocktail. BODDY and SCARLET engage in the following dialogue in italics only if SCARLET has been chosen as the killer. Otherwise, BODDY exits and the scene is played beginning with GREEN's entrance.)

SCARLET. *Mr. Boddy, what's the man of the house up to?*
BODDY. *(Magically presents a piece of sheet music.) Scarlet, what's this?*
SCARLET. *(Defensive.) Where'd you get that?*
BODDY. *In your chamber. (Pause. SCARLET looks dumbfounded and does not respond.) It's sheet music. (Sly.) What are you doing with this sheet music?*
SCARLET. *(Hesitant.) Uhm ... I'm singing it in my new act.*
BODDY. *Beethoven's Fifth Symphony?*

(SCARLET forces an unconvincing smile.)

SCARLET. *I'm in big voice these days. (Changes the subject.) You want a drink?*
BODDY. *(Sly.) I'll see you later.*

(BODDY exits.)

SCARLET. *(Mixing cocktail.)* I'll add a little vodka. A dash of gin. And a big splash of beer to mix it all together.
GREEN. That's some cocktail.
SCARLET. You want one?
GREEN. How about something a little less complicated? *(Moves close to SCARLET.)* Like a glass of water.
SCARLET. *(Moves away from GREEN.)* None bottled. And the water pipe in here is broken.
GREEN. *(Moves uncomfortably close to her.)* Wine. Mr. Boddy always has a decent bottle of wine lying around.
SCARLET. *(Abruptly turns away.)* In the cellar.

(BODDY makes the lead pipe magically appear. GREEN retrieves it.)

GREEN. I wouldn't call that a bottle of wine.

(BODDY makes the wrench magically appear. SCARLET retrieves it.)

SCARLET. Or that. A lead pipe and a wrench?
GREEN. Plumbing repairs, obviously. *(BODDY makes a bottle of wine magically appear. GREEN retrieves it.)* Here it is. *(Reading the label, he mispronounces the French, heavily Anglicizing it.)* Vine dee Paays.
SCARLET. *(Properly pronounces the French.)* Vin de pays. It's French country wine.
GREEN. Hey, you're good. Where'dya pick up the French ... Scarletta?
SCARLET. *(Surprised.)* How did you know my name?
GREEN. The last time I saw you, you were in Vegas beltin' out Sinatra tunes.
SCARLET. *(Caught off guard, nervous.)* I don't know you.
GREEN. You won the Miss Nuclear Waste Pageant.
SCARLET. Everyone knows that.
GREEN. 'Cause I paid off the judges!
SCARLET. Squeegy?!
GREEN. *(Thick Italian accent.)* Squeegy Sangilooni, in the flesh!

(BODDY, onstage and unseen by SCARLET and GREEN, waves his hand to propel SCARLET running toward GREEN. They embrace in a stylized manner, which evolves in and out of a using the following abstract sounds to emphasize each of their movements. BODDY exits.)

SCARLET and **GREEN.** Aaaaaaah! Uh. Uh. Uh. Brlrlrlrlrlrlrl.
SCARLET. I can't believe it. Look at you. What happened to the long hair, the stomach, the ten pounds of gold around your neck?
GREEN. If you want to be successful in business, you need a certain look, a certain sound. Now, I'm Mr. Green—*jack of all shades.* *(Beat.)* What about you?

SCARLET. *(With affectation.)* I'm a refined lady now. *Miss* Scarlet.

GREEN. Baby, a leopard doesn't change its "dese", "dems" and "dose".

SCARLET. You don't know. Squeegy. I've changed. I hated that way of life.

GREEN. As I recall, you didn't have it too bad. Nice apartment. Nice car. *(Referring to himself.)* Nice company.

SCARLET. Yeah, things were good. Until you left. Why'd ya split?

GREEN. You can't stick around when your two business partners, one who's your girl, itch up, and leave you in the dust.

SCARLET. I didn't know what Mr. Boddy was up to. Really. He only put the make on me to get access to the accounts. Then he drained them, leaving me and our business penniless.

GREEN. So, why are you here?

SCARLET. Why are *you* here?

GREEN. To right the wrong.

SCARLET. His wrong?

GREEN. His wrong. You with me?

SCARLET. You. Me. How?

(SCARLET and GREEN sing EVERYDAY DEVICES)

GREEN.
IT WAS VERY SELFISH WHEN
HE EXECUTED HIS INTENTION
    SCARLET.
MAKING US THE OBJECT OF
HIS DANGEROUS INVENTION
    SCARLET and **GREEN.**
BUT WE LOST NONETHELESS
PERHAPS WE MUST ADDRESS
A LITTLE RETRIBUTION
    GREEN.
METHODS, MEANS AND EXECUTION
ARE THE STRATEGIES THAT COUNT A LOT

SCARLET.
ACTING WITH EFFICIENCY
WILL GUARANTEE WE DON'T GET CAUGHT
   SCARLET and **GREEN.**
BUT WE LOST NONETHELESS
PERHAPS WE MUST ADDRESS
A LITTLE RETRIBUTION

EVERYDAY DEVICES
HAVE ENTERPRISING USES
WHEN THEY'RE IN THE RIGHT HANDS
BUT FOR THE WRONG REASONS
DELIGHTFULLY DELICIOUS
THESE DANGEROUS ABUSES
WHEN THEY'RE IN THE RIGHT HANDS
BUT FOR THE WRONG REASONS
   SCARLET.
IF WE WERE TO REALLY DO IT
ANY HOUSEHOLD ITEM
WOULD BE GOOD ENOUGH TO FIGHT HIM
   GREEN.
JUST AS LONG AS I'M WITH YOU
ANY GRISLY GADGET
WOULD MOST DEFINITELY DO

WE COULD WHIP HIM
   SCARLET.
YEAH, WITH AN EGG BEATER
   GREEN.
THEN MAYBE WE COULD WHACK HIM
   SCARLET.
WITH A WEED EATER
   GREEN.
LET'S STRING HIM, STRING HIM UP
   SCARLET.
I'VE GOT IT! WITH A TELEPHONE CORD
   SCARLET and **GREEN.**
WE COULD FLATTEN HIM

SCARLET and **GREEN.** (Cont.)
WITH AN IRONING BOARD

EVERYDAY DEVICES
HAVE ENTERPRISING USES
WHEN THEY'RE IN THE RIGHT HANDS
BUT FOR THE WRONG REASONS

IF WE WERE TO REALLY DO IT
ANY HOUSEHOLD ITEM
WOULD BE GOOD ENOUGH TO FIGHT HIM

JUST AS LONG AS I'M WITH YOU
ANY GRISLY GADGET
WOULD MOST DEFINITELY DO

*(GREEN and SCARLET exit. PLUM, PEACOCK, WHITE and MUS-
TARD enter and sing.)*

OTHERS.
STRANGULATE, OBLITERATE
WE LIQUIDATE THE OPPOSITION
EVALUATE, EXTERMINATE
WE ORCHESTRATE RETALIATION

FOR WE LOST NONETHELESS
PERHAPS WE MUST ADDRESS
A LITTLE RETRIBUTION
PLUM.
WE COULD PERFORATE HIM
PEACOCK.
YEAH, WITH A SILVER ICE PICK
MUSTARD.
WE COULD CRACK HIM
WHITE.
ON THE HEAD
PEACOCK.
WITH A HOCKEY STICK

PLUM.
WE COULD ROLL HIM
   MUSTARD.
WE COULD STUFF HIM

(GREEN and SCARLET reenter.)

   WHITE.
IN A TOOL BENCH
   ALL.
WE COULD THRASH HIM
WITH A MONKEY WRENCH

GREEN/SCARLET.	**OTHERS.**
EVERYDAY EVERYDAY DEVICES	EVERYDAY DEVICES
VERY ENTERPRISING ENTERPRISING	HAVE ENTERPRISING USES
USES WHEN THEY'RE IN IN THE HANDS OF	WHEN THEY'RE IN
ANYONE WHO KNOWS HOW BEST	THE RIGHT HANDS
TO USE THEM	BUT FOR THE WRONG REASONS
IF WE REALLY WERE TO DO IT	IF WE WERE TO REALLY DO IT
THEN ANY HOUSEHOLD ITEM	ANY HOUSEHOLD ITEM
WOULD BE GOOD ENOUGH TO FIGHT HIM	WOULD BE GOOD BE GOOD ENOUGH TO FIGHT HIM, AH
EVERYDAY DEVICES	OO-OO-OO-OO
HAVE ENTERPRISING USES	OO-OO-OO-OO
WHEN THEY'RE IN THE RIGHT HANDS	WHEN THEY'RE IN THE RIGHT HANDS
BUT FOR THE WRONG REASONS	BUT FOR THE WRONG REASONS

GREEN/SCARLET. (Cont.)	**OTHERS.** (Cont.)
DELIGHTFULLY DELICIOUS	AH, DELICIOUS
THESE DANGEROUS ABUSES	AH-AH-AH-AH
WHEN THEY'RE IN THE	WHEN THEY'RE IN THE
RIGHT HANDS	RIGHT HANDS
BUT FOR THE WRONG	BUT FOR THE WRONG
REASONS	REASONS
IF WE WERE TO REALLY	IF WE WERE TO REALLY
DO IT	DO IT
ANY HOUSEHOLD ITEM	AH-AH-AH-AH, FIGHT HIM
WOULD BE GOOD ENOUGH	
TO FIGHT HIM	

   ALL.
JUST AS LONG AS I'M WITH YOU
ANY GRISLY GADGET
WITH YOU
WOULD MOST DEFINITELY DO

(ALL exit except SCARLET and GREEN, who pose for the next clue. House Lights up. BODDY enters and speaks.)

BODDY.
Clue Number Four:
Wrench, pipe, lounge, Scarlet and Green—
In our conclusion, are any foreseen?
Consider one/none of the weapons here;
Consider one/none of the suspects here.
The lounge, well, future clues will reveal
If this is the scene of the deadly ordeal.

(Set changes to the study. House Lights fade out. PLUM enters and sits.)

BODDY. (Cont.)
Now in the study a fuss is made
Between one under stress and one underpaid.

(PLUM toes a noose during the following passage. BODDY mimes, in the shadows, as though he is controlling the actor.)

PLUM. Right over left, left over right, right under left and through the loop, left over right, through the loop and tighten. There. A perfect Achaen knot. Now, if I pull here I have a noose. A brilliant noose.

(WHITE enters. BODDY disappears.)

WHITE. Hey, that's me clothes line. You've cut it to bits!
PLUM. Not to worry. I shall replace it.
WHITE. *(Mimicking PLUM.)* Bet your sweet bottom you *shall*.
PLUM. You will.
WHITE. I will what?
PLUM. You will replace it.
WHITE. I ain't replacin' it. It's you what made a mess of it.
PLUM. Proper English: You *will* replace it.
WHITE. I will not. You bloody ruined it!
PLUM. It's not you shall; it's you will.
WHITE. Go ahead. Try and confuse me, so I forget about the rope and don't make you pay for it. You highfalutin types are all the same. You're a sly one, you are.
PLUM. Not as sly as your boss.
WHITE. You talkin' about Mr. B?
PLUM. The ace swindler himself.
WHITE. You got some dirt on 'im, ain't-cha?
PLUM. Dirt is a substance that lies on the face of the earth, and in your case, under your fingernails.
WHITE. Blimey!
PLUM. Yes, I have some information about Mr. Boddy.
WHITE. Oh do tell.
PLUM. I don't know if I can trust you, Mrs. White.

(WHITE grabs the noose and throws it over PLUM's neck.)

WHITE. You tell me, or you'll be sorry. You will.
PLUM. Very good, Mrs. White. *(Instructs like a school teacher.)* First person singular and plural, use shall. Second and third persons

singular and plural, use *will.*

WHITE. *(Impatient.)* You sound like a bloody school teacher. *(Tugs on the rope.)* Tell. Tell!

PLUM. *(Takes the noose off.)* As a businessman, Mr. Boddy intentionally acted to drive down the stock prices of certain oil companies, making them bankrupt. He then bought the companies at a disturbingly low price and sold them years later for an excessive profit.

WHITE. What's wrong with that? It's the American way.

PLUM. What's wrong is that the beneficiaries of corporate donations, like educational institutions, lose funding. They suffer. They suffer badly.

WHITE. What does it matter to you?

PLUM. I lost out.

WHITE. You're in business?

PLUM. *(Contriving an answer.)* Uhm ... business ... yes. One of the companies he ... uh ... drove into bankruptcy and then unfairly purchased was ... my family's business ... in Springfield, Massachusetts.

WHITE. What was the name of the company?

PLUM. *(Stalling at first.)* Uhm ... wh ... PTA.

WHITE. PTA?

PLUM. PTA ... O. Plum Trans Atlantic Oil.

WHITE. Oil in Massachusetts?

PLUM. Y ... Yes.

WHITE. Well, it looks like we got somethin' in common.

PLUM. Your family was in oil?

WHITE. Uh huh. Me dad had a fish and chips shop in the East End.

PLUM. Yes.

WHITE. Say, after what Mr. B's done, why are ya helpin' 'im with his book?

PLUM. The dignity lost to greed, I shall gain by proximity to the perpetrator. He'll pay with more than the author's advance he owes me.

WHITE. Oh, you're so poetic. I do like a sensitive bloke. Manly on the outside. *(Tickles him.)* Soft and squishy inside. You know, I get off work after dinner. What's say you and me take a moonlight stroll and get to know each other a little better?

PLUM. Mrs.. White, I think I know all there is to know.
WHITE. Yeah, I sorta wear me personality on me sleeve, don't I?
PLUM. *(Referring to her soiled apron.)* Actually, all over your apron.

(WHITE reacts with vehemence.)
(ONLY if PROFESSOR PLUM is the killer selected by the cards, conclude this scene with the dialogue in italics below, inserting it here, and omitting the final two lines proceeding this instruction.)

WHITE. I just came by to tell you that dinner will be ready shortly.

(WHITE exits.)

PLUM. Yes, dinner!

(PLUM exits.)

WHITE. *(Cont.) I just came by to give you this sheet music. I found it in your chamber when I was tidying up. (Reads title, mispronouncing it.) Hmm, Fifth Simfoney by Beethuvin.*
PLUM. *It's Beethoven! (Defensively grabs the music.) Give me that!*
WHITE. *You don't look very musical.*
PLUM. *You don't look very tidy.*
WHITE. *Dinner will be ready shortly.*

(WHITE exits.)

PLUM. *Yes, dinner!*

(PLUM poses. WHITE joins him onstage. House Lights up. BODDY enters and speaks.)

BODDY.
Clue Number Five:
Plum and White in the study with the rope—
Do any of these offer you hope?

BODDY. (Cont.)
None/One/Two/three of the four in the answer exist(s)
But maybe there's an unexpected twist.

(Set changes to the conservatory. House Lights fade. PEACOCK enters.)

BODDY. (Cont.)
The conservatory we visit now;
Here there's a saga of vow after vow.
(To PEACOCK.) My dear, it is imperative that we conclude our conversation from earlier.

(Use the following dialogue in italics only if PEACOCK has been chosen as the killer.)

BODDY. *(Magically presents a piece of sheet music.) And that you explain this.*
PEACOCK. *(Defensive.) Where'd you get that?*
BODDY. *In your night stand. (Pause. PEACOCK is dumbfounded and does not respond.) It's sheet music. (Sly.) What are you doing with sheet music to Beethoven's Fifth Symphony?*
PEACOCK. I don't like your tone.
BODDY. I don't like your reckless escapades.
PEACOCK. I've an insatiable spirit.
BODDY. *(Takes candlestick from her.)* Let me inform you, my dear, that I will not tolerate such displays of frivolous abandon.
PEACOCK. Let me inform you, my dear, that you may not have to.

*(BODDY reacts and exits. PEACOCK sings **ONCE A WIDOW**.)*

PEACOCK.
SOME WOMEN WED FOR LIFE
AT TIMES I DISPARAGE
MY HIST'RY OF MARRIAGE
HAS BEEN MATRIMONIAL STRIFE

A WOMAN IN MY PRIME

I MARRIED OLD MONEY
SO OLD IT'S NOT FUNNY
FORGET ABOUT PASSION
HOW VERY OLD FASHIONED
MY FIRST ONE THEN DROPPED DEAD
ON THE NIGHT WE WED

ONCE A WIDOW
OH THEY BLAMED ME
YES THEY NAMED ME
AS THE SCHEMING SPOUSE
BUT THE JUDGE, HE, SET ME FREE
MY DEFENSE WAS INSANITY

THE JUDGE AND I THEN WED
THE GOSSIP DISTRESSED ME
BUT THE COULDN'T ARREST ME
THE NIGHT MY POOR JUDGIE DROPPED DEAD

A THIRD ONE WAS A SHRINK
A REAL LADY KILLER
HIS DEATH WAS A THRILLER
I GET SENTIMENTAL
IT WAS RULED ACCIDENTAL
THE INQUEST WAS ROUTINE
IT PLACED ME AT THE SCENE

TWICE A WIDOW
THEY DEFAMED ME
THRICE A WIDOW
OH THEY LOATHED ME MORE
SO I MARRIED THE ATTORNEY FOR THE SHRINK
ONTO NUMBER FOUR

MY LAWYER WAS A CHARM
BUT HE SQUANDERED MY ASSETS
AND LEFT ME SOME BAD DEBTS
THEN SUDDENLY HE BOUGHT THE FARM

PEACOCK. (Cont.)
MY FIFTH ONE MADE NO SENSE
THE ROMANCE WAS FLEETING
THEN I CAUGHT HIM CHEATING
YOU CAN ASK ANY JURY
A SCORNED WOMAN'S FURY
IS GROUNDS FOR SELF DEFENSE
MY FIFTH IS NOW PAST TENSE

WHEN THEY THROW RICE
I SHOULD THINK TWICE
I'M A WOMAN WITH FIVE MEN ON ICE
FIVE TIMES WIDOWED
WHY DID THEY BLAME ME
IT'S THE PRICE THAT I PAY
CAUSE I'VE HAD MORE THAN ONE WEDDING DAY
AND WHEN FIVE PASSED AWAY
THEY CRIED FOUL PLAY

(House Lights up. PEACOCK poses. BODDY enters and speaks.)

BODDY.
Clue Number Six:
Let us consider the conservatory,
Where Peacock's tale was every man's story.
It certainly could house the deadly deed,
And/But the cards have/haven't given us that exact lead.

(Beat. House Lights down.)

Now we waltz so my guests will know
I have no qualm with my potential foe.
Murder is fated, not by chance,
And is now set in motion with the dance!

*(BODDY approaches PEACOCK. There is a moment of silent recon-
ciliation, then they ease into a waltz. The OTHER CHARACTERS
join in the waltz one at a time. At the end of the waltz, each re-*

trieves a cordial glass.)

BODDY. Ladies and Gentlemen, I trust you all enjoyed dinner, and that you are pleasantly satiated. I have asked all of you, including Mrs. White, to join me in an after-dinner cordial, because you are a collection of varied personalities with a single objective: my demise. *(OTHERS reacts with cacophonous ad-libs.)* Yes. *(Ad-libs cease.)* Revenge, diversion, pleasure, pain ... whatever your motivation, each of you wants me dead.

ALL. *(Except BODDY.)* *(With a whisper/chant effect.)* Dead.

BODDY. *(To audience.)* Don't look so sad. I live to be killed. *(Laughs deviously, then addresses the characters.)* I want you all to know that I will cooperate fully, so that your individual needs will be met. What you must do is plan your strategy wisely. Only the correct combination of suspect, room and weapon will result in the successful murder of me, in winning the game! *(With pomp.)* You know the ends you must individually achieve. I now offer a toast to your success. Raise your glasses. *(ALL raise glasses.)* May the best murderer win. *(MUSIC in.)* To success.

ALL. Success.

(The CHARACTERS look at each other on musical accents, then exit.)

*(BODDY sings **CORRIDORS AND HALLS**.)*

BODDY.
RESTIVE SPIRITS ROAM
ALL THROUGHOUT THE NIGHT
THEY SEARCH THROUGH EVERY ROOM
WHICH ONE'S RIGHT
WHICH ONE WILL BE MY
RESTING PLACE TONIIII ...

(BODDY hits a sour note, because he notices something wrong with piano.)

BODDY. What's the matter? The piano suddenly sounds terrible.

(Light on PIANIST.)

PIANIST. A key is broken.
BODDY. It sounded fine up until now.
PIANIST. I was playing around it.
BODDY. Well, continue playing around it.

(BODDY resumes singing the verse.)

BODDY.
WALK TO A DOOR
DARE TO STEP THROUGH

(BODDY claps. The SUSPECTS enter and pose.)

TRUTH LIES INSIDE
WELL-HIDDEN FROM VIEW

(BODDY claps. The SUSPECTS move, then sing.)

SUSPECTS.
NOT EVERY ROOM
WILL FIT THE BILL
ONE'S MARKED FOR DEATH
IT'S TIME TO KILL

(BODDY exits.)

CORRIDORS AND HALLS
A WINDING HIDDEN STAIR
A SECRET PASSAGEWAY
LEADS SOMEWHERE

EACH ROOM'S SO RARE
A TRUE WORK OF ART
WITH TRAP DOORS IN THE FLOORS
AND BOOKSHELVES THAT PART

CORRIDORS AND HALLS
A MANSION FULL OF DOOM
ONE OF US MUST CHOOSE
ONE CORPSE, ONE ROOM

DINING ROOM CHAIRS
MOVE IN THE NIGHT
LIGHT SWITCHES OFF
LIGHTS SHINING BRIGHT

WHERE WILL WE GO
FEAR EVERYWHERE
DON'T LOOK BEHIND
SOMEONE IS THERE

(The following lines are spoken.)

    GREEN. There.
    PLUM. There.
    WHITE. There.
    SUSPECTS. *(Continue singing.)*
CORRIDORS AND HALLS
A WINDING HIDDEN STAIR
A SECRET PASSAGEWAY
LEADS SOMEWHERE

EACH ROOM'S SO RARE
A TRUE WORK OF ART
WITH TRAP DOORS IN THE FLOORS
AND BOOKSHELVES THAT PART

CORRIDORS AND HALLS
A MANSION FULL OF DOOM
ONE OF US MUST CHOOSE
ONE CORPSE, ONE ROOM
    PEACOCK.
THE BILLIARD ROOM

GREEN.
WHERE ALL THE PORTRAITS STARE
  WHITE.
AND THE WALLS
  MUSTARD.
ALL HAVE EARS
  SCARLET.
IT COULD CURL YOUR HAIR
  SUSPECTS.
WHEN THE DEED
IS COMPLETE THIS NIGHT
SEE THE PAST COME TO LIFE
WHAT A SIGHT

THE LIBRARY DOORS
OPEN BY THEMSELVES
PULL OUT A BOOK
AND YOU MOVE THE SHELVES

ALL THE BEDROOM FLOORS
CREEK TO A BEAT
WITH NO ONE WALKIN' CROSS
AND NO ONE'S FEET

CORRIDORS AND HALLS
A MANSION FULL OF DOOM
ONE OF US WILL CHOOSE
ONLY ONE CAN LOSE
ONLY ONE CORPSE
ONE ROOM!

(At the end of the song, the CHARACTERS stand in two parallel lines. With the following lines of dialogue, each refers to BODDY, who is positioned USC.)

SCARLET. You shouldn't have dumped me.
PEACOCK. You shouldn't have been so rude.
GREEN. You shouldn't have cheated me.

MUSTARD. You shouldn't have married my love.
PLUM. You shouldn't have swindled my family.
WHITE. You shouldn't have been so cheap.

*(Segue to ... **THE MURDER**)*

(Sinister, yet humorously mysterious music underscores the very styl-ized murder of BODDY. The stage is alive with vigorous, fun-filled choreography, as the SUSPECTS pursue BODDY in and around the mansion with the Clue weapons. All suspect/room/weapon combinations are illustrated, e.g. Mrs. Peacock in the conservatory with the candlestick; Mr. Green in the billiard room with the rope, etc. There is a blackout during which the following dialogue is spoken—refer to score.)

PEACOCK. There he is.
WHITE. No, there he is.
MUSTARD. There he is.
SCARLET. Here?

(SE: Thunder and Lightening.)

GREEN. Where?
PLUM. There.
WHITE. There.
PEACOCK. There.
SCARLET. Where?
SUSPECTS. There. There. There!

(Choreography leads into the SUSPECTS chasing BODDY, eventu-ally closing in on him.)

SUSPECTS.
Wrench, candlestick, pipe
Knife, revolver, rope
Wrench, candlestick, pipe
Knife, revolver, rope
Wrench, candlestick, pipe

Knife, revolver, rope

(The frenzied action peaks, as thunder sounds and lightning bolts flash. Then, the SUSPECTS part. There lying on the floor dead, is BODDY.)

*(SUSPECTS Sing **AFTER THE MURDER (THE GAME Reprise)**)*

SUSPECTS.
AND NOW THE HEAT IS ON TO FIND A KILLER
FOR MURDER ONE IT'S ALL OR NONE
WE PLAY THE GAME TO WIN.
YES WE ...
JUST PLAY THE GAME
PLAY THE GAME
PLAY THE GAME TO WIN.

(Lights out on CAST; bright on Confidential envelope. Then back up on CAST. With a musical crescendo, BODDY stands and addresses the audience.)

BODDY.
Now, I am dead. *(Beat.)*
My anticipated fatality
Is all in the line of duty
So, please, no sympathy.
Let's move ahead.

Round one is ended;
Two will now begin.
In this round there'll be three clues
To ponder and to muse,
To advance you to a win.

From what you've witnessed, it's hard to surmise
The who, where and how surrounding my demise;
So to make your theorizing more effective
I offer you an expert, bona fide detective!

(BODDY gestures grandly. The SUSPECTS' tableau opens to reveal the DETECTIVE, as she enters. BODDY exits.)

DETECTIVE. I'm a hard-nosed detective, whose hard pressed to find the hard truth. I'm tough on crime, tough to talk to, and tough as nails. I turn over stones, turn over suspects and turn over when I sleep. My direct questions get direct answers. For me, yes means yes, no means no, and maybe means you're under the influence of an illegal substance. Peter may have picked a peck of pickled peppers, and she may have sold sea shells by the sea shore, but everywhere that Mary went *this* lamb *won't* be going. Is that clear? *(DETECTIVE turns to see SUSPECTS are staring at her. She is suddenly insecure and unusually vulnerable.)* What are you all staring at?

WHITE. Miss, there's been a murder.

DETECTIVE. *(Strong again.)* I know.

GREEN. What do you mean, you know?

DETECTIVE. I've searched the premises. Mr. Boddy's body is missing. And you all have horrendous expressions of guilt on your faces.

PEACOCK. Excuse me, but my plastic surgeon fixed that.

SCARLET. Why are you here? None of us called a detective.

DETECTIVE. I'm supposed to be here.

MUSTARD. You're not in the instructions.

DETECTIVE. Who reads instructions?

GREEN. I bet you're a lost token from Sorry.

(SUSPECTS cackle.)

PLUM. Or better yet, she's a discarded token from Life.

(SUSPECTS laugh.)

WHITE. You better leave.

SCARLET. This is not Life.

SUSPECTS. SOR-RY!

(SUSPECTS all laugh and ad-lib ferociously. BODDY regains order with his chant.)

BODDY.
Wrench, candlestick, pipe
Knife, revolver, rope.
DETECTIVE. That's better. *(Beat.)* Now, who here knew Mr. Boddy? *(Looking at her, SUSPECTS diligently raise their hands.)* Everybody. Who here wanted a dead Mr. Boddy? *(SUSPECTS drop their hands.)* Nobody. Well, we will see.
PLUM. We *shall.*
DETECTIVE. We shall what?
PLUM. Forget it.
SCARLET. I want you to know, here and now, that I am not guilty. Murder is too vulgar.
DETECTIVE. Like your social life, I'm sure.
MUSTARD. *(Fun, robust.)* Colonel Mustard here. I like how you charge in and take control. Together we'll find the killer. We'll take down the enemy. *(He puts his arm around MRS. WHITE for solidarity. Then he pauses, dumbfounded.)* Why do I have my arm around a bulldozer?
DETECTIVE. Retreat, Colonel.
PEACOCK. Detective, certainly you don't think that I could ... *(DETECTIVE glares at PEACOCK.)* How much do you want to drop the whole thing?
DETECTIVE. I'm glad I don't have your nerve in my tooth.
PLUM. It surely wasn't I. I get my jollies from crossword puzzles, not cold corpses.
WHITE. That's not what I hear. *(Beat.)* And don't look at me, Detective. I hate murder.
PLUM. Because you can't spell it.

(WHITE and PLUM argue with ad-libs. OTHERS join in.)

DETECTIVE. That's enough. *(Beat.)* You know, now that I look at you chumps in your wardrobe by Crayola, I doubt that any of you have the right stuff to be a murderer. Mr. Boddy's death was probably caused by natural causes ... dice failure, card trauma ... whatever. I think I'll be on my way.

(The SUSPECTS are noticeably surprised that DETECTIVE is leaving, and robbing them of the opportunity to be in the lime light as the game's killer.)

PEACOCK. Just a minute. A murderer is a select individual, someone with style. I *breathe* style.

DETECTIVE. I have a feeling all you breathe is fire.

MUSTARD. A killer is stouthearted. Just call me Gibraltar. I don't waiver. I don't flinch. I ... *(HE notices GREEN staring at him.)* What is that gigantic string bean staring at me?

PLUM. The mind that plots and executes a murder is an extraordinary one: immense intelligence, superior IQ. Consider me.

SCARLET. No me. A killer requires creativity and passion. It's an art. I'm a true artist. I work with Minsky's Mongrels.

DETECTIVE. What do you do with the mongrels? *(Beat.)* Don't answer that.

GREEN. A killer is a sharp strategist. Sharp, that's me ... sharp as a thimble.

WHITE. A killer is unique. Detective, I'm unique.

DETECTIVE. You certainly are. But, let's stick to the subject of murder. Shall we?

PLUM. Very good.

DETECTIVE. What?

PLUM. Forget it.

DETECTIVE. So, these little piggies are innocent. Then these little piggies are not. Well, one of you little piggies is gonna go wee-wee-wee all the way home, 'cause I'm stickin' around, and I'm gonna figure this out. *(Strong.)* I suspect that each of you had a motive to kill Mr. Boddy, and I'm gonna wanna question you. *(To GREEN.)* All of you!

GREEN. Babe, if you think you're lookin' at a killer, clean the wax out of your ears.

DETECTIVE. *(Feisty.)* Now, I'm in charge. And I'm gonna huff and I'm gonna puff and I'm gonna make sure one of you gets life.

PEACOCK. Behind bars?

DETECTIVE. In the box!

SUSPECTS. *(Ad-lib boisterously.)* Oh no! Not life in the box! How horrible! Etc.

DETECTIVE. Now my investigation formally begins. You are all suspects! *(She sees the SUSPECTS intently staring at her. Her veneer of power disappears. She is vulnerable.)* Why are you staring at me?

(DETECTIVE exits. SUSPECTS sing SHE HASN'T GOT A CLUE.)

PLUM.
SHE'S A MASTER OF DETECTION
  PEACOCK.
AND DETERMINED TO DELIVER
  GREEN.
IF WE PLAY OUR CARDS WRONG
WE'RE REALLY UP THE RIVER
  PEACOCK.
SHE IS HARD-BOILED
  MUSTARD.
COMMANDEERING
  PLUM.
QUITE ATTRACTIVE
  SCARLET.
AND DISARMING
  WHITE.
BUT THE SIGHT OF PRISON STRIPES
IT AIN'T SO CHARMING
  PEACOCK.
SHE'LL TRY TO CATCH US IN A LIE
  GREEN.
HER ACCUSATIONS WON'T HOLD GLUE
  ALL.
IF WE DON'T HANG TOGETHER NOW
TOGETHER WE WILL HAND ON CUE
  SCARLET and **GREEN.**
SHE'S AMBITIOUS
  PEACOCK and **PLUM.**
UNRELENTING
  MUSTARD.
OUT TO SOLVE THIS DEADLY THRILLER

WHITE.
BUT SHE CAN'T EVEN FIND THE CORPSE
MUCH LESS THE KILLER
   ALL.
PREMEDITATE OUR EVERY MOVE
ELIMINATE THE SLIGHTEST CLUE
CHASING HER TAIL FROM ROOM TO ROOM
BUT SIMPLE STRATEGY WILL SEE US THROUGH

SUSPECTS AND VILLAINS
NO CORPSE YET, JUST KILLIN'
THEORIES AND LAYING BLAME
WITH NO CLUES, WE CAN'T LOSE
IT'S A DARK, DEADLY GAME
IT'S JUST A GUESSING GAME

DINNER, INVITE US
DESSERT, THEN INDICT US
PRISON'S THE BILL OF FARE
IF WE SCARE, SO BEWARE
ALIBIS MUST COMPARE
   WHITE.
I DIDN'T
   ALL EXCEPT MUSTARD.
HE WASN'T
   ALL EXCEPT SCARLET.
SHE WOULDN'T
   ALL.
WE COULDN'T

THERE'S NOTHING THAT SHE CAN PROVE
AND SHE HASN'T GOT A CLUE

*(The following lines are spoken. The part of the line in italics is de-
livered more loudly than the other, so that the italicized part is
clearly audible, and the remaining part creates an aural texture,
which crescendoes into cacophony—only to be resolved by singing again.)*

PEACOCK. *Could she have found out ...*
that I had Mr. Boddy's lawyers add special fine print his will *(then ad-libs.)*
MUSTARD. *Does she know about ...*
the time I convinced Mr. Boddy that he was a toaster *(then ad-libs.)*
SCARLET. *Has she learned about ...*
Mr. Boddy used me to extort funds from my business with Squeegy *(then ad-libs.)*
PLUM. *Would she have discovered ...*
the story about my family's business going under is false *(then ad-libs.)*
WHITE. *Did she stumble on ...*
Mr. Boddy's deal with me son Nigel.
GREEN. *Can she be aware ...*

(Ad-libs cease with musical cue. ALL sing.)

   ALL.
SUSPECTS AND VILLAINS
NO CORPSE YET, IT'S CHILLIN'
THERE ARE PLENTY OF THEORIES
THERE IS PLENTY OF BLAME

WITH NO CLUES, WE CAN'T LOSE
IT'S A DARK, DEADLY GAME
IT'S JUST A GUESSING GAME
   MEN.
PLAY THE GAME
   PEACOCK. *Could she ...*
   MUSTARD. *Does she ...*
   SCARLET. *Has she ...*
   PLUM. *Would she ...*
   WHITE. *Did she ...*
   GREEN. *Can she ...*

(ALL sing.)

ALL.

DINNER INVITE US TO DINNER INVITE US	DINNER, INVITE US
THEN DESSERT US AFTER DINNER	DESSERT, THEN INDICT US
AFTER DINNER INDICT US	

PRISON'S THE BILL OF FARE
IF WE SCARE, SO BEWARE
ALIBIS MUST COMPARE
   WHITE.
I DIDN'T
   ALL EXCEPT MUSTARD.
HE WASN'T
   ALL EXCEPT SCARLET.
SHE WOULDN'T
   ALL.
WE COULDN'T

THERE'S NOTHING THAT SHE CAN PROVE
AND SHE HASN'T GOT A CLUE

(SUSPECTS end in a tableau. On applause, they move upstage ad-libbing, quietly. BODDY enters. House Lights up.)

BODDY.
The investigation now underway—
I present to you
The first clue
of Round Number Two:

Focus on where the deed was executed
When to calm my vigor was transmuted.
The room which housed the deliberate act
(Insert the one appropriate line below.)

Study:	Had misunderstanding, fun and fact.
Ballroom:	Had velvet draped and rival attacked.

Conservatory: Had verdant hue the others lacked.
Kitchen: Had motive tossed and bovine whacked.
Billiard Room: Had threats and ultimatums racked.
Lounge: Had libations mixed and strategies stacked.

(House Lights out.)

    The suspects now learn
    That the detective
    Is quite effective
    And far more clever
    Than any of them ever
    Thought she could be.

(DETECTIVE enters and takes center. A table comes in to center stage. Note: it is important that the staging of this section go from methodical to frantic, but always remain in control.)

DETECTIVE. So ... *(SUSPECTS' Ad-libs cease.)* You think I haven't got a clue. I've got a lot more. This itsy bitsy spider crawled up more than the water spout. I searched the entire mansion. And I found these. *(BODDY presents a bag, which DETECTIVE grabs, not acknowledging BODDY's presence.)* Six interesting items, which I believe could easily have been used to commit the heinous crime I'm faced with solving. *(As she speaks, she takes the weapons out of the bag, and presents them. BODDY stands to the side and observes.)* I found a revolver in the ball room, a wrench in the kitchen, a coil of rope in the lounge, a candlestick in the billiard room, a knife in the conservatory, and a lead pipe in the study. *(Beat.)* With my highly advanced, lap-top crime detection system, I was able to ascertain that *all* of your fingerprints appear on *all* of the items. *And* that the prints were made between 9:00 PM and the precise moment of Mr. Boddy's death, midnight.
    PLUM. Don't go any further. I maintain my innocence. Therefore, I will admit of my own free will that I did indeed handle three of those weapons, but not for the grisly crime of murder. After dinner at 9:02, I moved the candlestick, when discovering it lying on its side in the library, I set it upright. At 9:11 I handled the revolver,

when I took it out of its display case in the study to inspect its caliber, merely out of curiosity. And, at 9:20 I used the knife in the kitchen to cut the rot out of an apple I was eating.

DETECTIVE. Those weapons were not found in those rooms.

PEACOCK. I was responsible for moving two of them. At 9:11, before I retired to my chamber, I saw Professor Plum handling the revolver and got suspicious, so I waited until he went to the kitchen and at 9:22 I moved it to a place where anyone with questionable motive could not find it, the conservatory, behind a lovely Wisnewski fern. At 9:30 I took the knife out of the kitchen and used it in the lounge to cut a twist for my martini.

DETECTIVE. You handled no others?

PEACOCK. Well, I did retrieve the wrench from the tool shed for the big, burly handy man, who needed it in the kitchen to work a pipe—a lead pipe.

DETECTIVE. At what time?

PEACOCK. When you're with a big burly handy man, you don't take notice of the time. *(Beat.)* It didn't stay in the kitchen, though, the wrench, that is. AT 9:44 I saw Mrs. White retrieve it.

WHITE. I needed it to get the cop off me new bottle of spirits, what I hides in the study behind some German book about outdoor recreation.

DETECTIVE. The name of the book.

WHITE. My Camp! *(Beat.)* At 9:50 I went to the lounge, so's I could finish me spirits like a proper lady, and I found the rope, which I lost on me way to the conserv'try.

DETECTIVE. *(Corrects WHITE's cockney pronunciation.)* The conser*vatory*?

WHITE. Yeah, to talk to the plants.

MUSTARD. I found the rope in the lounge at 9:58. Mrs. Peacock promised we would play Cowboys and Indians. And you can't play Cowboys and Indians without a rope.

DETECTIVE. *(Sarcastic.)* You certainly can't.

MUSTARD. I used the lead pipe in the kitchen at 10:23 to crack open a can of rations.

DETECTIVE. You still eat that stuff?

MUSTARD. Rations stay with you forever.

(MRS. WHITE burps. ALL react.)

SCARLET. At 10:30 I took the wrench to the handy man in the ballroom, who needed it to fix a radiator.

DETECTIVE. That handy man is quite popular. Huh, ladies?

GREEN. At 10:40 I gave him the knife in the lounge to cut his bologna sandwich.

DETECTIVE. More popular than I thought. *(Beat.)* Is that it?

PEACOCK. No *(Beat.)* I then retrieved the candlestick for some night reading in the study. 10:50.

WHITE. Then I brought it to the conserv'try for some atmosphere. 10:55.

PLUM. I took it the billiard room to experiment with playing pool. 11:00 (eleven.).

SCARLET. I carried it to the ballroom to catch the view from the balcony. 11:05.

MUSTARD. I tot he lounge for a romantic rendezvous with Mrs. Peacock. 11:10.

GREEN. And I to the kitchen for a late snack. 11:15.

MUSTARD. I took the revolver out of the conservatory. 11:20.

PEACOCK. Then I hid it in the billiard room. :22 (twenty-two).

PLUM. I carried it to the ballroom. :24

SCARLET. I took it in the kitchen. :26.

GREEN. I had it in the study. :28.

WHITE. And I in the lounge. :30.

SCARLET. The rope ...

PEACOCK. To the billiard room.

MUSTARD. The conservatory.

GREEN. The study.

PLUM. The ballroom.

WHITE. The lounge.

PEACOCK. Wrench.

PLUM. Kitchen.

GREEN. Billiard room

MUSTARD. Study.

SCARLET. Ballroom.
WHITE. Lounge.

SCARLET. Knife.
PLUM. Billiard room.
GREEN. Ballroom.
WHITE. Lounge.

MUSTARD. Pipe
GREEN. Kitchen.
PEACOCK. Study.
WHITE. Lounge.

SCARLET. Rope
PLUM. Conservatory.
WHITE. Lounge.

PEACOCK. Wrench.
GREEN. Study.
WHITE. Lounge.

SCARLET. Candlestick.
WHITE. Lounge.

PLUM. Revolver.
WHITE. Lounge.

PEACOCK. Rope.
WHITE. Lounge.

GREEN. Knife.
WHITE. Lounge.

MUSTARD. Pipe.
WHITE. Lounge.

BODDY. *(Regains control.)* Wrench.
WHITE. Lounge.

BODDY. Candlestick.
WHITE. Lounge.
BODDY. Pipe.
WHITE. Lounge.
BODDY. Knife, revolver, rope.
SUSPECTS.
Wrench, Candlestick, pipe
Knife, revolver, rope
Wrench, candlestick, pipe
Knife, revolver, rope

(SUSPECTS sing EVERYDAY DEVICES (Reprise)

SUSPECTS.
EVERYDAY DEVICES
HAVE ENTERPRISING USES
WHEN THEY'RE IN THE RIGHT HANDS
BUT FOR THE WRONG REASONS

DELIGHTFULLY DELICIOUS
THESE DANGEROUS ABUSES
WHEN THEY'RE IN THE RIGHT HANDS/IN
THE RIGHT, IN/HANDS THE RIGHT HANDS
THE RIGHT, IN THE RIGHT
IN THE RIGHT HANDS

*(By now each SUSPECT is in possession of a weapon and is very
    impassioned.)*

WRENCH AND PIPE
KNIFE AND ROPE
EVERYONE'S A CLUE
AND ANY GRISLY GADGET

DETECTIVE. You people act like you're out of a board game!
ALL.
WOULD MOST CERTAINLY DO
(Shouted.) Midnight!

(SUSPECTS end in a tableau, with weapons held high.)

DETECTIVE. Well ... *(SUSPECTS break tableau and look at DETECTIVE.)* I'm not finished. This Jack is still at the top of the beanstalk. And she's got something else on you! *(Presents note with gusto.)* This note! It's made form magazine cut-outs and it reads: It's My Turn! Hmm. I'm convinced more than ever that one of you is guilty of murder. And I'm going to find that person! I'll be interrogating all of you shortly. *(Beat, Insecure.)* Stop staring at me.

(DETECTIVE exits. SUSPECTS deliver the following lines, as they exit.)

WHITE. She's so frazzled.
GREEN. Serious.
MUSTARD. Charged.
SCARLET. Shrewd.
PEACOCK. Tacky.
PLUM. Attractive.

(BODDY is alone. House Lights up.)

BODDY.
Information is essential—
I present it to you
The second clue
Of Round Number Two:

Focus on how the deed was completed—
How I, with all glory, was fatally defeated.
The weapon responsible for killing me
(Insert to one appropriate line below.)

Revolver:	The world's fastest feet might never flee.
Knife:	Traverses its intended cunningly.
Pipe:	Has no smoke, but is indeed deadly.
Candle:	With ornate design commits treachery.
Rope:	Secures a victim sinuously.
Wrench:	Can turn a crime most brilliantly.

(House Lights out.)

BODDY. (Cont.)
Now, to the library.

(Music in. BODDY speaks as the Set changes to the Library. DETEC-TIVE enters with a chair and sets in center stage. PLUM sits.)

BODDY. (Cont.)
Here the detective conducts her interrogation;
The suspects distress with each accusation.
She is alert,
Bold, cunning and curt;
They desperately jockey for vindication.
DETECTIVE. Professor Plum. *(Lighting effect. PLUM poses.)*
Tell em, could a savvy person such as yourself commit the crime of murder, simply because his family's oil business was betrayed?
PLUM. Could I? Yes. Did I?

(PLUM laughs.)

DETECTIVE. I read your book on corruptions in the CIA. Rather enjoyed it. *(Inquisitive.)* You know, you look different than in the photo on the book jacket.
PLUM. *(Uneasy.)* Film can never capture exact likeness.
DETECTIVE. Very different. *(Pause.)* I read somewhere that you were now in South America, working on a book about ...
PLUM. *(Changes the subject.)* Let me give you some advice, my sharp detective. A sophisticated criminal act is best deduced with patience, astute reasoning and ... cocktails for two. What do you say you join me for a drink?
DETECTIVE. I have a murder to solve.
PLUM. Come on. Let two master minds spin stimulating conversation.
DETECTIVE. Stimulation is not in my job description.
PLUM. Do as the great minds of ages past would. Imbibe with me. Converse with me. Fertilize my cerebral garden.
DETECTIVE. I gave up fertilizing cerebral gardens, when my shrink

told me that fertilizing rose gardens was a healthier choice for a bi-polar co-dependent, who regresses to her childhood for emotional support.

PLUM. As Somerset Maughm said, "The mind is most free when the body is satiated with pleasure."

DETECTIVE. As Emerson said, "The eye of prudence may never shut."

PLUM. "The awful thing about most people is their caution." Thomas Wolfe.

DETECTIVE. "He has not desire for that of which he feels no want." Euripides.

PLUM. *(Coming on to her.)* "The only way to get rid of temptation is to yield to it." Oscar Wilde.

DETECTIVE. "I desire only to know the truth." Euripides.

PLUM. "Beauty is truth—truth, beauty. That is all ye need to know." Keats.

DETECTIVE. "Let one be on guard against those who flatter and mislead." Aristotle.

PLUM. *(With gusto.)* "Make yourself necessary to somebody." Emerson. "Be not simply good; be good for something." *(Big come on.)* Thoreau—oh—oh!

DETECTIVE. *(Skeptical.)* Oh?

*(PLUM and DETECTIVE sing **SEDUCTION DEDUCTION**.)*

PLUM.
CRIMINAL PROPENSITIES
AND CALCULATED RISKS
    DETECTIVE.
MOTIVE, OPPORTUNITY
POISON AND PLOT TWISTS
    PLUM.
MADE FOR PRIME-TIME THRILLERS
CRIMES OF PASSION. ALIBIS
    DETECTIVE.
WE'RE CONSUMED BY BLOOD AND GUTS
    PLUM.
BUT IN THE NEWS ROOM MURDER FLIES

IT'S NORMAL CURIOSITY
TO THRILL AT THE NOTION
OF ENGAGING IN FOUL PLAY
   DETECTIVE.
BUT IN CIVILIZED SOCIETY
WE STIFLE THAT EMOTION
IN FEAR OF JUDGMENT DAY
   PLUM.
TELL THE TRUTH, YOU'RE SEDUCED BY MY THEORY
YOUR CAREER FILLS A NEED DEEP WITHIN
MISCHIEF FILLS THE MINDS OF MORE THAN KILLERS
YOU'RE BEWITCHED BY THE DEADLY SCENT OF SIN
   DETECTIVE.
I ENJOY AMASSING MODUS OPERANDI
I'M ENTRANCED BY EXPLORING BRUTAL ACTS
YES, A CRIMINAL'S CONFESSION'S CAPTIVATING
BUT NOT COMPARED TO DISSECTING MANIACS
   BOTH.
CRIMINAL PROPENSITIES
AND CALCULATED RISKS
MOTIVE, OPPORTUNITY
POISON AND PLOT TWISTS

MADE FOR PRIME-TIME THRILLERS
CRIMES OF PASSION, ALIBIS
WE'RE CONSUMED BY BLOOD AND GUTS
BUT IN THE NEWS ROOM MURDER FLIES

(Dance: Tango. Insert the following dialogue.)

   PLUM. Thoreau: "Don't be too moral ...
   DETECTIVE. "You may cheat yourself out of much life. *(Beat.)*
Aristotle: "If he have not virtue ...
   PLUM. "He is the most savage of all animals."
   DETECTIVE. Yes!

(DETECTIVE throws herself at PLUM.)

PLUM.
TELL THE TRUTH, YOU'RE SEDUCED BY MY THEORY
YOUR CAREER FILLS A NEED DEEP WITHIN
MISCHIEF FILLS THE MINDS OF MORE THAN KILLERS
YOU'RE BEWITCHED BY THE DEADLY SCENT OF SIN
   DETECTIVE.
I ENJOY AMASSING MODUS OPERANDI
I'M ENTRANCED BY EXPLORING BRUTAL ACTS
YES, A CRIMINAL'S CONFESSION'S CAPTIVATING
BUT NOT COMPARED TO DISSECTING PSYCHOPATHS
   BOTH.
THE DESIGN OF THIS GAME
IS NOT MERELY TO ENTERTAIN
(IT'S) COMING IN FOR THE KILL
THAT EXCITES ME

WE'RE SEDUCED BY THE CHALLENGE
THEN REDUCED TO THE CHASE
ON THE HELLS OF HOT PURSUIT
   DETECTIVE.
TO PROSECUTE
   PLUM.
TO EXECUTE
   BOTH.
AN OPEN AND SHUT CASE!
   DETECTIVE. *(Regrouping.)* No more questions.

(PLUM smiles and exits. MUSTARD enters and takes a seat.)

   DETECTIVE. (Cont.) Colonel Mustard

(Lighting effect. MUSTARD poses.)

   DETECTIVE. You certainly have an appetite for murder. When Mr. Boddy's father passed legislation banning you from the military, you offed him.
   MUSTARD. No, I went off *with* him.
   DETECTIVE. To a remote village in Honduras, where he was

slaughtered during tribal ritual and fed to the gods. Then, you married Mr. Boddy's mother, who weeks later was found dead with a noose around her neck.

MUSTARD. In Cowboys and Indians, the rules say losers must hang themselves. I didn't know she'd take me seriously.

DETECTIVE. In her will, she left you the house. There was nothing Mr. Boddy could do about this. The inheritance was yours legally. But a betrothed Mrs. Peacock, you could never claim. So it was your turn. You killed Mr. Boddy because he married your one true love to avenge you.

MUSTARD. For the death of his parents? For owning his home?

DETECTIVE. *(Big.)* No. Because when he was a child you convinced him he was a toaster!

(MUSTARD sings FOUL WEATHER FRIEND, bribing DETECTIVE with military prowess.)

MUSTARD.
ALL THESE MEDALS ON MY CHEST
MADE THE SOLDIER YOU SEE
I KNOW, YOU MUST BE IMPRESSED
I SEE HOW YOU LOOK AT ME

I'LL TRADE YOU ALL THIS GLORY
IF YOU CHANGE YOUR STORY
VINDICATE ME, EXONERATE ME
ALLIES IN THE BATTLE, IT'S WAR!

(MUSTARD exits. GREEN enters and takes the seat.)

DETECTIVE. Mr. Green. *(Lighting effect. GREEN poses.)* You're a conniver, you're a chauvinist, you're a snake.

GREEN. No, I'm a Democrat.

DETECTIVE. You've been a business partner of Mr. Boddy in several ventures. With the one in Vegas, he swindled you out of a bundle.

GREEN. Hey, that's the way the cookie bounces.

DETECTIVE. With Colossal Nips and Tucks the roles were reversed. It was your turn. You were duping him out of hundreds of thousands of dollars. He found out. Threatened you. You killed him.

GREEN. Look, that money was mine. I know. Because I never count my chickens before the cross the sidewalk. *(Beat.)* And Babe, if you think I'm a killer, you're tryin' to fit a round peg into a bread box.

(GREEN sings, bribing DETECTIVE with cash.)

GREEN.
CHEATS AND THIEVES
BLUE-COLLAR CRIME
THAT'S JUST NICKEL AND DIME

CHECK MY COLLAR
GREEN'S MY GAME
NOTHING BUT THE BIG TIME

I'VE BEEN 'ROUND THE BLOCK TWICE
NOT AFRAID TO TOSS DICE
TAKE MY MONEY
COME ON HONEY
BRIBIN' AND CONNIVIN'S MY WAY!

(GREEN exits. SCARLET, PEACOCK and WHITE enter and position themselves around the center chair.)

DETECTIVE. Here we go, Ladies. *(Lighting effect. LADIES pose.)* You first. *(SCARLET sits.)* Miss Scarlet. So, your real name is Scarletta Vermicelli.

WHITE. I'll have mine al dente.

(WHITE laughs raucously at her own joke.)

DETECTIVE. Please. *(Back to SCARLET.)* You were hooked up with Mr. Boddy in Vegas. He used you to extort funds form a business you, he and Mr. Green had. Then he dumped you.

SCARLET. The bum proposed marriage and everything.

DETECTIVE. Did such betrayal spur revenge here and now?

Was it your turn? Did you kill him?

SCARLET. *(With passion.)* I got my revenge in Vegas. I caught Mr. Boddy at the airport, dragged him back to town ...

WHITE. And tortured him?

SCARLET. Yes! I made him sit through Suzanne Sommer's night-club act ...

(PEACOCK gasps.)

SCARLET. And Applaud!

(ALL react as SCARLET rises. WHITE sits.)

DETECTIVE. Mrs. White. Did you kill Mr. Boddy to erase your step-son Nigel's debt? *(WHITE is silent.)* No, you killed him because he was driving you like a slave. It was your turn! *(WHITE is silent.)* Mrs. White, what are you hiding?

WHITE. Whatever it is, it's well-hidden.

DETECTIVE. If Mr. Boddy's death was caused by a blow to the head, which it may have been, the killer would have to have been tall. How tall are you?

WHITE. *(Stands.)* Six, three. (or correct height.)

DETECTIVE. With heels?

WHITE. With anyone.

(WHITE moves aside. PEACOCK sits.)

DETECTIVE. Mrs. Peacock. Five husbands, Five questionable deaths. Five fortunes, now yours. And according to the fine print your lawyers added to Mr. Boddy's will, upon his passing, you inherit his entire estate.

PEACOCK. Remember something, Detective. With a lawyer who makes more an hour than you make in a week, it's *always* my turn!

(PEACOCK stands. SCARLET, PEACOCK, and WHITE sing.)

SCARLET, PEACOCK and **WHITE.**
SILVER BULLETS WITH YOUR NAME

IF YOU CUT US A DEAL
DIAMOND HANDCUFFS, PLAY OUR GAME
PROMISE WE'LL NEVER SQUEAL

WE SHOULD STICK TOGETHER
FEMALES IN FOUL WEATHER
PLEASE DON'T SELL US DOWN THE RIVER
ROWIN' UP WITHOUT AN OAR.

TAKE OUR RINGS
AND IF YOU LIKE 'EM
WE'LL GET MORE

PRETTY THINGS
WE'LL GET WHATEVER
YOU ADORE
ON THE MAKE 'TIL THE END
FOUL WEATHER FRIEND

(GREEN and MUSTARD enter and sing.)

GREEN.
NEVER KNOW WHO'S 'ROUND THE BEND
   MUSTARD.
IS IT OUR FOUL WEATHER FRIEND
   SCARLET, PEACOCK and WHITE.
HE'S SUSPICIOUS
   MUSTARD and GREEN.
SHE'S MALICIOUS
   ALL.
TWO-FACED TO THE END

(PLUM enters and joins the group.)

   ALL.
ALL IS FAIR IN LOVE AND WAR
MURDER SETTLES THE SCORE
EACH OF US COULD WALK SCOTT-FREE

WE COULD OFFER YOU MORE

(To one another.)
WE SHOULD STICK TOGETHER
COMRADES IN FOUL WEATHER
(To DETECTIVE.)
PLEASE DON'T SELL US DOWN THE RIVER
ROWIN' UP WITHOUT AN OAR

BEAT THE WRAP
IF WE CAN CHEAT 'EM
WE CAN BEAT 'EM

TAKE OUR CASH
WE'LL MAYBE SQUEAL
OR CUT A DEAL
ON THE MAKE 'TIL THE END
FOUL WEATHER FRIEND

NEVER KNOW WHO'S 'ROUND THE BEND
IS IT MY FOUL WEATHER FRIEND
HE'S SUSPICIOUS, SHE'S MALICIOUS
TWO-FACED 'TIL THE END
STICK TOGETHER
IN FOUL WEATHER
MY FOUL WEATHER FRIEND

(SUSPECTS and DETECTIVE remain in their tableau. BODDY enters. House Lights up.)

BODDY.
Ladies and Gentlemen
I present to you
The final clue
of Round Number Two:
The game continues, not yet complete;
Deducing the answer no easy feat.
The suspect you should scrutinize

(Insert the one appropriate line below.)

Peacock:	Has deliberate moves and altered eyes.
Plum:	Has insightful moves and curious eyes.
Scarlet:	Has brazen moves and dazzling eyes.
Mustard:	Has playful moves and attractive eyes.
White:	Has awkward moves and busy eyes.
Green:	Has cunning moves and scheming eyes.

(House Lights out.)

DETECTIVE. Well, well, well, well, well, well. *(Each SUSPECT peals away from position to upstage.)* Rub-a-dub-dub, six suspects in a tub ... full of hot water. Your secrets are out in the open. I could pin this murder wrap on any of you if I wanted to. But only one of you did it. And I've got the proof! *(Each SUSPECT exits as s/he is accused.)* Was it Mrs. White in the ballroom with the candlestick? Or ... Mrs. Peacock in the billiard room with the knife. Or ... Professor Plum in the conservatory with the revolver? Or ... Miss Scarlet in the study with the rope? Mr. Green ... Colonel Mustard ... Yeah, run. Run fast. Jack be nimble, Jack be quick, but Jack can't out run this maverick!

*(Staging brings the SUSPECTS back onstage, as they sing **DON'T BLAME ME**.)*

WHITE. *(To GREEN.)*
GREEN MEANS YOU'RE FULL OF ENVY
    PEACOCK. *(To SCARLET.)*
SCARLET SHOWS A JEALOUS STREAK
    PLUM.
THEIR COLORS ARE THE MOTIVE
    PEACOCK, WHITE and **PLUM.**
FOR TWO KILLERS CHEEK TO CHEEK
    SCARLET.
YOUR ASSUMPTIONS ARE INSANE
    GREEN.
AND WE'RE AS CLEAN AS YELLOW SNOW

MUSTARD.
PLUM'S THE ONE THAT'S TALL ENOUGH
  MUSTARD, SCARLET and **GREEN.**
TO STRIKE THE FATAL BLOW
  PLUM. *(To GREEN.)*
FOR A BUCK, YOU LOST YOUR LUCK
  MUSTARD. *(To WHITE.)*
FOR YOUR SON, YOU PACKED A GUN
  PEACOCK. *(To SCARLET.)*
FOR LOST LOVE, YOU'LL GO TO JAIL
  GREEN. *(To SCARLET.)*
YO! HERE'S FIVE BUCKS TOWARD YOUR BAIL
  BODDY. *(To SUSPECTS.)*
IT'S ALL MY FAULT YOU'RE IN THIS MESS
I CRAVE THE CHANCE TO DIE
THE JOY OF IMMORTALITY
I'M CORPUS DELECTI
  GREEN and **SCARLET.** *(To PEACOCK and MUSTARD.)*
YOU BOTH CONSPIRED TO KILL HIM
YOU'RE TWO LOVERS WITH A SCHEME
ILLICIT ASSIGNATIONS
YOU'RE THE PERFECT MURDER TEAM
  WHITE. *(To PEACOCK.)*
DON'T BLAME ME, SHE'S IN THE WILL
  PEACOCK. *(To WHITE.)*
DON'T FRAME ME YOU FIT THE BILL
  PLUM. *(To WHITE.)*
YOU'LL HANG HIGH WHEN I TESTIFY
  SUSPECTS. *(To AUDIENCE.)*
AYE, IT'S ME THEY'RE GONNA FRY
  BODDY.
A CORPSE LEADS TO A KILLER
  DETECTIVE.
BUT A KILLER HANGS HIMSELF
  BODDY and **DETECTIVE.**
THEY'VE STRAYED FROM THE COMMANDMENT
"LOVE THY NEIGHBOR AS THY SELF?

DETECTIVE.
IT'S ALL YOUR FAULT YOU'RE IN THIS MESS
BUT SOON YOU'LL PAY YOUR DUES
EXCUSE ME MR. GREEN
COULD THOSE BE BRUNO MAGLI SHOES?
   DETECTIVE.
BY DESIGN, IT'S CHECKOUT TIME
   BODDY.
MY DEMISE, THE PERFECT CRIME
   DETECTIVE and **BODDY.**
TOSS THE DICE, THE FINAL ROLL
ROLL WITH NO HOPE FOR PAROLE
   SUSPECTS. *(To AUDIENCE.)*
IT'S ALL YOUR FAULT WE'RE IN THIS MESS
WE'RE SORRY THAT YOU CAME
SO NEXT TIME PLAY PARCHEESI
PLEASE JUST FIND ANOTHER GAME
   ALL.
NOW MAKE YOUR ACCUSATION
AND BE SURE THE CLUES ALL FIT
BUT IF THERE IS A SHRED OF DOUBT
YOU KNOW YOU MUST ACQUIT

DELIBERATE, DON'T SPECULATE
IMPLICATE, ELIMINATE
LAY THE BLAME
   SUSPECTS.
BUT NOT ON ME
CAST YOUR VOTE AND SET ME FREE

(Musical Interlude.)

   BODDY. *(To AUDIENCE.)*
Complete your form
The time is now
You must select
Who, where and how

(ALL onstage busily ad-lib during the musical interlude, as the audience completes their playing forms. There is a sense that at this point we are putting the final pieces of the mystery, the game and the musical together; therefore, if required, the set units are returned to their original positions.)

ALL.
DELIBERATE, DON'T SPECULATE
IMPLICATE, ELIMINATE
CAST YOUR VOTE AND SET ME FREE
PLAY THE GAME—BUT DON'T BLAME ME!

(ALL end in a tableau.)

DETECTIVE. Hickory dickory dock, soon one of you will be behind a lock ... and key ... and bars ... with no window ... and bad food ... and mean guards ... *(She breaks into maniacal laughter. BODDY joins in laughing. SUSPECTS stare at DETECTIVE, alarmed. Then, she speaks confidently, defiantly.)* Stare at me all you like. I'll be back for you shortly.

*(BODDY sings **THE FINAL CLUE.**)*

BODDY.
SHE'S A MASTER OF DETECTION
AND DETERMINED TO DELIVER
SHE'S UNCOVERED EVERY CLUE
THAT WE HAVE GIVEN HER

ALL PIECES FIT TOGETHER
NOW THAT SUSPECTS WONDER WHETHER
   SUSPECTS.
WE'RE OFF TO A PRISON PEN
BIRDS OF A FEATHER

WE'RE ALL BEHIND THE EIGHT BALL NOW
SHE HAS US CORNERED LIKE A RAT
SHE CLAIMS SHE KNOWS, WHO, WHERE AND HOW

EVERY ALIBI HAS FALLEN FLAT

WE'RE OUT OF ROOMS TO HIDE IN NOW
TIME'S RUNNING OUT TO LAY THE BLAME
WE'RE OUT OF ROOMS TO HIDE IN NOW
TIME'S RUNNING OUT TO LAY THE BLAME

*(As the Music continues, the DETECTIVE reenters. MR. BODDY
hands her the Confidential envelope from the podium. With
BODDY's assistance the DETECTIVE removes the three cards
inside and ritualistically scrutinizes each, backs to the audience.
At the Music's conclusion, she announces with fortitude ...)*

DETECTIVE. It was (person)! In the (room)! With the (weapon)!

*(BODDY takes the envelope and cards, places the envelope on the
easel so that "Confidential" faces away from the audience and exits with the cards, as the MURDERER comes forward and con-
fesses.)*

*(**CONFESSIONS**—Only ONE per performance, as determined by
the cards.)*

PEACOCK. Yes, yes, I did it. I killed Mr. Boddy in the (room)
with the (weapon), because love is a four letter word; money is a five
letter word, and more is better. With him dead, his fortune is mine!
Mine! Mine!

— OR —

PLUM. Yes, yes, I did it. I killed Mr. Boddy in the (room) with
the (weapon), because he never paid me my author's advance, and as
Thomas Fuller said, "God makes, and apparel shapes, but it's *money*
that finishes the man."

— OR —

SCARLET. Yes, yes, I did it. I killed Mr. Boddy in the (room), with the (weapon), because on the night he proposed, before he dumped me, he game me a ring. It wasn't diamond. It wasn't ruby. It wasn't sapphire. It was cubic zirconia ... paste ... garbage. Nobody treats this lady like a five-and-dime dame and lives to revisit the pawn shop.

—OR—

GREEN. Yes, yes, I did it. I killed Mr. Boddy in the (room), with the (weapon), because he cheated me. Well, he's repaid that debt. Mr. Boddy's the first client in my new chain of upscale cemeteries: Last Stop of the Rich and Famous. Our motto: You're the tops, six feet under.

— OR —

WHITE. Yes, yes, I did it. I killed Mr. Boddy in the (room), with the (weapon), because with him dead, me boy Nigel is free on bail, and I don't have to work me fingers to the bone any more to pay his debt. So the calluses on me calluses won't grow more calluses! Happy days is here again!

— OR —

MUSTARD. Yes, yes, I did it. I killed Mr. Boddy in the (room), with the (weapon), because when he stole Mrs. Peacock from me, he stole the passion that made this man an emotional hero. Without her, I'm just a common foot soldier marching down love's empty trail. Onward ho ... oh-oh-oh.

(MUSTARD weeps.)

(THEN ... BODDY enters with a list of audience members, who guessed correctly the game's conclusion. House Lights Up.)

BODDY.
Let's see who in the audience won the game.
Whose conclusions with our's were one in the same

Please rise in your place
With a smile on your face
If you guessed the right room, weapon and name.

(Winning AUDIENCE MEMBERS stand.)

Let's have a round of applause for our winners.

(AUDIENCE MEMBERS sit. DETECTIVE comes forward. BODDY exits.)

DETECTIVE. Not so fast. (Suspect) did it all right. Sort of. S/he certainly had motive to want Mr. Boddy dead. But s/he was only the accomplice. The actual killer was ... Professor Plum!
 PLUM. You're mad. I am no killer.
 DETECTIVE. I did not say you were. I said Professor Plum was.
 PLUM. I am Professor Plum. BA, MA, PhD ... that's me.
 DETECTIVE. Oh no you're not.

(In the event the PLUM is the killer selected by the cards, replace the underlined dialogue above with the italicized dialogue below, then continue with the dialogue as written.)

* **PLUM.** You're mad!*
* **DETECTIVE.** Oh, no I'm not. And you're not Professor Plum!*

DETECTIVE. (Cont.) You're no internationally renowned author. You're no PhD. You're not MA. You're barely a BA. You're a dorky school teacher from Springfield, Massachusetts, who came here disguised as Professor Plum, because you had a bone to pick with Mr. Boddy. He drove the businesses into bankruptcy, which funded your private school. With no money, your school closed, and you lost your job as English teacher and head of the PTA. PTA! Not Plum Trans Atlantic. Parents Teachers Association! But you didn't kill him. You're too much of a wimp. Anyone who seduces a woman with Thoreau is a wimp!

(PLUM, embarrassed, whimpers and retreats US.)

DETECTIVE. Ladies and Gentlemen, the murder scenario was this. The real Professor Plum killed Mr. Boddy, because Boddy had repeatedly demoted him—from prime player int eh game, to secondary suspect, to mere spectator, and then to the most demeaning of all positions ...

(The PIANIST a/k/a the real Prof. Plum, hits the piano keys in a resounding dissonance and stands form behnd keyboard. He wears a costume or costume pieces identical to PROF. PLUM.)

PIANIST. Piano Player! (Music: He plays the four signature chords form Beethoven's Fifth Symphony.) Mr. Boddy would not acknowledge that I could play the game as well as the others, that I had real talent for murder, so I had to show him. (Evil laugh.) Yes, yes, yes! It was my turn! I did it in the (room), with the (weapon), and (declared murderer)/that imposter was my accomplice. S/he supplied me with the weapon and made sure there were no witnesses. (To DETECTIVE.) How did you get me?

(BODDY enters with physical evidence concealed. As DETECTIVE announces each piece below, BODDY gives them to her, and She displays them to the audience.)

DETECTIVE. There were three crucial bits of evidence. One linked you to the accomplice: the sheet music! One supplied the motive of revenge: the note made from magazine cut outs! And, the clue that told me it was you and only you: the broken piano key!

(BODDY exits, while SUSPECTS meet center stage, furiously; ad-libbing: "I told you s/he was guilty."; "With a (weapon), how ingenious."; "Just an accomplice." etc. Then GREEN spots DE-TECTIVE leaving.)

GREEN. Hey ... (ALL quiet.) Where are you going?
DETECTIVE. This game is too complex and dangerous. I'm off to play another one. No maladjusted psychopaths. No intricate motives. No murder. *(BODDY has reentered and gives her the game Monopoly, which she presents to the audience.)* Just railroads and hotels.

SUSPECTS. *(With disdain and fright.)* MONOPOLY!!!

(DETECTIVE exits.)

PEACOCK. You know, her idea is a good one. I wouldn't mind getting out of here and spending some time in Palm Beach. I'll give Teddy Kennedy a call and see if his offer is still good.

PLUM. I would like to find myself in a more erudite setting: a Tony Kushner play, a John Fowles novel—where I'd be in a complex plot with an enlightened them, interacting with characters of depth.

SCARLET. I could see myself out of this tired old mansion and in something significant and deep, too—like a Muppet Movie/John Waters' Film.
(The Director should choose which of the two films would be most appropriate for the audience.)

MUSTARD. I'll rise through the ranks to become a global leader, a beacon of hope for the masses. I'll see a new world order. I'll see a bright tomorrow! *(He executes a grand movement, causing his plastic vertebrae to stick.)* Aaah! I'll see a chiropractor.

WHITE. A holiday to me homeland on the QEII. Six days crossin' the Atlantic with hunky stewards tendin' to me every need. *(Sultry.)* I mean every need.

GREEN. I wouldn't mind a Caribbean trip to the Greek Islands.

BODDY.
Wrench, candlestick, pipe
Knife, revolver, rope

SUSPECTS. *(Joining in one at a time.)*
Wrench, candlestick, pipe
Knife, revolver, rope

BODDY. *(To AUDIENCE.)*
You see, some things must remain the same
Our game has been played
It is over, this merry escapade
Until once more we lift the cover
And sift through clues to discover
The mystery source from whence they came

(BODDY gives an evil laugh.)

*(ALL sing **THE GAME (Finale)***

ALL.
EACH TIME YOU PLAY OUR LITTLE GAME OF MURDER
YOU TRY YOUR BEST AND PLAY THE GAME TO WIN
AND NO MATTER IF YOU LAND ON TOP OR BOTTOM
YOU'VE PLAYED IT
AND TURN AROUND AND PLAY THE GAME AGAIN.
YES, SO NOW THE GAME IS DONE
SIX SUSPECTS ON THE RUN
IT'S ALWAYS ALL OR NONE FOR MURDER ONE

(Lights out. ALL exit.)

(BOWS.)
(CURTAIN CALL)

(SHE HASN'T GOT A CLUE (Reprise)

ALL.
DINNER, INVITE US
DESSERT, THEN INDICT US
PRISON'S THE BILL OF FARE
IF WE SCARE, SO BEWARE
ALIBIS MUST COMPARE

I DIDN'T
HE WASN'T
SHE WOULDN'T
WE COULDN'T

(The following dialogue is optional. If it is not used, sing SHE HASN'T GOT A CLUE Reprise with no interruption.)

(BODDY notices that the percussion is off, and stops the song.)

BODDY. Stop. Stop. The rhythm is off. What's wrong?

(Light on PERCUSSIONIST.)

PERCUSSIONIST. *(Stands.)* A mallet is broken.

(ALL on stage look at one another and gasp.)

ALL.
THERE'S NOTHING THAT YOU CAN PROVE
IF YOU HAVEN'T GOT A CLUE!

END OF PLAY

Audience Participation Plays and Musicals

By **Tom Chiodo** and **Peter De Pietro**

MURDER AT RUTHERFORD HOUSE
BROADWAY BABYLON

By **Tom Chiodo**

BOARDWALK MELODY HOUR MURDERS
DEADLY HABIT
THE END OF THE LINE
THE MEDIEVAL MURDERS
MURDER UNDER THE BIG TOP

By **Peter DePietro**

DEATH AND DECEIT ON THE NILE
DEATH SUITE
DEDICATED TO THE END
FATAL COMBINATION
THE HILARIOUS HILLBILLY MASSACRE
MURDER AT THE PROM

For information on complete production packages, see the
Samuel French Basic Catalogue of Plays and Musicals